THE ONLY BLACK GIRLS IN TOWN

THE ONLY BLACK GIRLS IN TOWN

BRANDY COLBERT

LITTLE, BROWN AND COMPANY

New York   Boston

Copyright © 2020 by Brandy Colbert

Cover art copyright © 2020 by Erin Robinson. Cover design by Marcie Lawrence and Jenny Kimura. Cover copyright © 2020 by Hachette Book Group, Inc.

Little, Brown and Company
Hachette Book Group
1290 Avenue of the Americas, New York, NY 10104
Visit us at LBYR.com

First Edition: March 2020

Little, Brown and Company is a division of Hachette Book Group, Inc. The Little, Brown name and logo are trademarks of Hachette Book Group, Inc.

The publisher is not responsible for websites (or their content) that are not owned by the publisher.

Library of Congress Cataloging-in-Publication Data
Names: Colbert, Brandy, author.
Title: The only black girls in town / by Brandy Colbert.
Description: New York ; Boston : Little, Brown and Company, 2020. | Summary: In a predominately white California beach town, the only two black seventh graders, Alberta and Edie, find hidden journals that uncover family secrets and speak to race relations in the past.
Identifiers: LCCN 2019022183| ISBN 9780316456388 (hardcover) | ISBN 9780316456371 (ebk.) | ISBN 9780316456395 (library edition ebk.)
Subjects: | CYAC: Friendship—Fiction. | African Americans—Fiction. | Race relations—Fiction. | Secrets—Fiction. | Gay fathers—Fiction. | California—Fiction.
Classification: LCC PZ7.C66998 Onl 2020 | DDC [Fic]—dc23
LC record available at https://lccn.loc.gov/2019022183

ISBNs: 978-0-316-45638-8 (hardcover), 978-0-316-45637-1 (ebook)

Printed in the United States of America

LSC-C

10 9 8 7 6 5 4 3 2 1

For all the Alberts in my family
And Great-Great-Aunt Alberta, too

BLENDING IN

I WOULD BE SAD THAT TODAY IS THE LAST DAY OF surf camp if I weren't so busy trying to ignore the worst person alive.

Our instructor, Irene, just passed out the trophies. Everyone got one, of course. They all say the same thing at the bottom: EWING BEACH SURF CAMP with the year engraved underneath. There's a tiny gold surfboard sitting on top.

Next to me, Nicolette McKee is repeatedly kicking the balls of her feet into the sand, trophy held slack at her side. I have to see her at school and all over town because Ewing Beach is tiny. And then there's the fact that she lives across the street, so I also have to see her just about every day of my life. But the end of surf camp means the start of school, and Nicolette is always worse when she's around her friends.

Irene stands in front of the whole group to say how much she's going to miss us. "I hope you'll all come to the end-of-summer party this weekend," she says, readjusting the knot of red hair on top of her head. "We're gonna grill out, and we'll have ice cream, and you can all bring your boards if you'd rather catch some waves."

Nicolette sneers. "These aren't even gold-plated," she mutters. "They're probably going to turn green in, like, a month."

On the other side of me, Oliver Guzman holds his trophy in the air, admiring it. "Where are you gonna put yours, Alberta?"

"In my room," I say, trying to ignore Nicolette. "What about you?"

"Our trophy case." He shrugs when I give him a look. "My parents are into it. They like to show it off when family comes over."

We all give ourselves a hand, Irene's favorite way

to close out each day of camp. Nicolette unzips her wet suit and starts pulling her arms out, right and then left. I bend down to slip my trophy into my bag, and when I stand up, Irene is in front of me.

"Great work this summer, Alberta," she says, her blue eyes warm.

"Thanks, Irene."

Then she smiles and leans in, whispering, "You were the best one in camp, but don't tell anyone I said that."

What? I barely have time to smile back before she's moving down the sand toward her assistant, Jed, who's breaking down the cardboard boxes that had held the trophies.

Irene was quiet, but by the grin Oliver gives me, I know he heard. And I really hope he was the only one. Even if Nicolette didn't hear Irene, she can probably *see* it on me. I can't stop grinning, and my chest immediately puffed up with pride as Irene's words sank in. I watch Irene as she talks to Jed and then wanders away, but she doesn't go up to anyone else and whisper in their ear.

"Awww." Nicolette's head is tilted to the side

as she looks at me with wide eyes. "That's cute, Alberta."

I know not to take the bait, but I do it anyway. "What?"

"That Irene tries to make you feel good about yourself here. I guess it's not like school, huh?"

I frown at her. I should walk away, but, like always, there's something inside me that plants my feet to the ground and makes me keep listening to Nicolette McKee. I hate that something.

Out of the corner of my eye, I see Oliver watching us.

"Sorry," Nicolette says, not looking sorry at all. "It's just that you're, like, different here and different *there*, but Irene tries to make it special for you. That's cute."

I've been coming to surf camp since I was six years old. Three hours a day, four days a week for two months. I don't need camp to surf, but it's more fun to be with people who love it as much as I do. And I am into everything about it except the fact that Nicolette is in my surf group. She'll take any chance to remind me that I don't look like other people in Ewing Beach—that she doesn't think I fit in.

I haven't said anything. Just like my feet are rooted in the sand, my lips are glued tightly together.

Nicolette pauses then blinks at me, her eyes even bigger. "I mean, do *you* think you were the best surfer in camp?"

Dad says not to respond to ignorance with ignorance, and I *know* it's never worth getting into it with Nicolette—ever—but sometimes I really want to.

"Yes," I finally say. "I do think I was the best. I guess you just aren't as good as you think you are."

My father would probably count that last part as an ignorant comment, but it's worth it just to see the way Nicolette's eyes narrow into the thinnest slits. And to hear Oliver snicker.

"Whatever, Alberta." She runs a hand over her wet ponytail, wringing out the last drips of water as she glares at me.

That—and she—is not even worth a response. I turn my back to her, tuck my board under my arm, and look at Oliver. "Ready?"

He nods and we head off together on our walk home, still wearing our wet suits. Oliver lives two blocks over from mine, and not for the first time,

I wish he were the one who lived across the street instead of Nicolette.

"What's her problem?" Oliver says, shaking his head.

I sigh. "I've been trying to figure that out for years."

"You competing in the Pismo contest this year?"

"Maybe." I hesitate. It's a very hopeful maybe. I'm not allowed to compete in surfing contests until I turn thirteen. My dads' rule, which I think is ridiculous. The contest is in a few weeks, and I don't turn thirteen until next year. But I'm hoping to convince them with my powers of persuasion. "What about you?"

"Nah, not really my thing. I mean, I like surfing, but soccer's more my sport."

By the time we reach my street, my arm is cramping from holding my board. Maybe it's because it's the last day of camp, but I feel more exhausted than I have all summer. I say good-bye to Oliver at the corner and cross the street by the bed and breakfast that sits across the road from our house. Everything looks the same as always: the same HARRIS INN sign swinging from the white wooden posts in front of the porch, the same avocado tree, its branches heavy with fruit, and—

Wait. There's a car in the driveway, and it's not the silver one that the realtor drives. And the FOR SALE sign is gone, the one that's been sitting in the yard for the last two months.

Someone bought the B&B? My stomach gets those excited flutters that mean something big is about to happen. Who's going to move in? I can't imagine anyone living there but Mrs. Harris.

Next to the B&B, little Stephan McKee is jumping up and down on his front porch, shouting at his nanny to hurry up so they can go to the beach. I roll my eyes. Stephan is five years old, and he's the biggest brat I know. He's always talking to his nanny like he's the one in charge, and his parents never tell him to be nicer. I guess that's no surprise, considering he's Nicolette's brother. Elliott says the entire family is cold.

Oliver and I rinsed our boards under the beach shower before we headed home, so I take mine around back to let it finish drying. Then I peel off my wet suit, hold it under the water spigot off the side of the house, and hang it to drip-dry in the shade.

When I walk around back, the door is open, letting in the breeze and letting out the sounds of Dad making lunch. I leave my surf bag on the porch, but I take out my trophy so I can put it next to the others in my room.

"How was it?" Dad asks as I kick off my sandy flip-flops and step inside. He's busy chopping up cucumbers for the quinoa salad, but he stops when he sees my trophy. "Hey, look at that!"

"It's not a big deal, Dad. *Everyone* got one." I pad barefoot across the kitchen and give him a kiss on the cheek. "But...Irene said I was the best surfer in camp."

Dad hoots with joy. "Of course she did! Of course you were. Good job, sweetheart. And not just because it means we're getting our money's worth out of that camp." He winks at me. "Can we put this one on the mantel?"

"Maybe," I say, turning it around in my hands. Even though it doesn't seem important enough to go in the front room. Not like the ones you actually earn, like in the Pismo contest. "I'm going to take a shower before we eat."

As much as I believe what Irene said, I wish I could remember it without thinking of Nicolette, too. I don't think anyone besides Oliver heard Irene, but I wonder if they'd believe the same thing. That Irene only said that to make me feel special.

I go to wash off all the sweat, sand, and salt, then meet Dad back in the kitchen where he's just finishing up the salad.

I grab two bowls in one hand and two glasses with another. Then I bump the cabinet door closed with my elbow. "Somebody bought the bed and breakfast?"

"Oh, I meant to tell you—I spoke to the real estate agent yesterday," Dad says, nodding. "The new owners just got here this morning."

After Mrs. Harris died, her grown kids arrived in three different cars, taking out boxes and boxes of stuff. Then construction workers started showing up every day, wearing fluorescent vests and hard hats as they did renovations. Everyone in town thought maybe one of Mrs. Harris's kids would take over the bed and breakfast, especially her daughter who lives here in Ewing Beach: Mrs. Palmer. But Dad says she's not interested in running a B&B, and the other two kids live across the country and don't want to move to California.

The real estate agent has shown it to a few people, but no one has lived or stayed there since June. It's the end of August now, which means the new owners are moving in just at the end of the busy season. Once the tourists stop coming, Ewing Beach looks like a ghost town.

"Do you know anything about the new neighbors?" I ask, putting silverware next to our bowls as Dad brings the salad to the table. I love quinoa salad. Unlike my best friend, Laramie, who says it feels like chewing on bugs. Laramie's family doesn't eat a lot of grains . . . or salad. Their mom works a bunch, and they eat a lot of fast-food burgers and mac and cheese from the box and her brother's culinary concoctions, which are only edible about half the time.

"I was trying not to be too nosy," Dad says, spreading his napkin over his lap.

I do the same. "You didn't find out *any*thing?"

"Well, I found out two things that *may* be of interest to you," he says in a singsongy voice that drives me crazy. He only uses it when he's trying to prolong the suspense, and it always ends up being more annoying than intriguing.

I take a bite of salad and wait for him to go on. He really drags it out, chewing another couple of bites. When he takes a drink of water and then dabs the corners of his mouth with a napkin, I can't take it anymore.

"*Dad!* What did you find out?"

He laughs. "Okay, okay. Well, I think it will be of great interest to you that, number one, the new neighbors have a girl just your age."

I nearly drop my fork on the floor. "What? *Really?*"

There hasn't been anyone my age on this street since we've lived here. And we've been here since I was two years old. I'm twelve now. It doesn't take long to get anywhere in Ewing Beach, but having a friend right across the street is something I've wished hard for and never expected to happen. Well, there's Nicolette, but she's a year older and definitely not a friend.

"Yup, she'll be in seventh grade next week, just like you."

I keep picking up forkfuls of quinoa, but I'm too excited to eat. I have a billion questions. Questions I am sure Dad doesn't know the answer to, like what is her name and can she surf and is she a vegetarian, too? But there is one more that he *can* answer.

"What's the other thing you know about them?" I ask. "You said there were two things."

"Ah, yes. Are you ready?"

"Dad." I give him my most exasperated look. It's not as good as Elliott's, but I think it's close.

"They're black!" he says in a voice so boisterous he sounds like the announcer on *The Price Is Right*— Elliott's guilty pleasure.

"What?" I frown, sure that I didn't hear him right.

"Finally, we won't be the only ones on the street."

Which means that *finally*, I won't be the only black girl in my entire grade.

I rinse the dishes before I put them in the dishwasher, making sure to not leave a bit of food on the bowls or silverware. My other dad, Elliott, is picky about the kitchen, from the way the dishwasher is loaded to how the glasses are lined up in the cabinet (the lip of the glass should be down, not up).

As I scrub quinoa from the bowls, I think about the new neighbors. There aren't many black people in Ewing Beach—barely any besides me, Dad, and Elliott. There are two boys a year older than me and a girl in the grade above them, but I'm the only black student in my grade. All the other black people in town are the same age as my grandparents and dads, or they're little kids who toddle around on the beach with diapers under their swimsuits. Even most of the tourists are white.

And now we'll have black neighbors? One who is a girl the same age as me? I have an overwhelming urge to find out everything about her. But Dad says we need to wait until tomorrow to introduce ourselves. Give them some time to settle in.

I have plans with Laramie, anyway. Her brother is working at the ice-cream shop today. She texted earlier and said I should come downtown because he always gives us a free cone when he's there.

I stick my head in the office/guest room. "Okay if I go down to meet Laramie at the creamery?"

Dad's frowning at his computer screen, but his worried eyebrows go back to normal when he looks at me. "Of course," he says. "Just promise you won't get butter pecan."

"Why wouldn't I? I like it." Which means I know I'll never be disappointed.

He groans and looks to the ceiling. "How did I end up raising a daughter so set in her ways? Have you seen the flavors they're getting in down there lately? Balsamic swirl! Strawberry rhubarb! Olive oil!"

I scrunch up my nose. "No, thank you."

Dad and Elliott are foodies, and I like most of the stuff they make, but I don't try new things very often. And I'm okay with that.

"Fine," he says with a sigh. "Guess I'll have to live vicariously through someone a bit more adventurous."

"Bye, Dad."

"I'm heading over to the gallery soon. Make sure you're back before dinner, Alberta," he calls after me.

I wheel my mint-green beach cruiser around the front of the house and look once more at the B&B before I push off. The car is still in the driveway, but I don't see anyone outside. I think back to the Fourth of July, when the construction workers and real estate agent were gone, and Laramie and I tried to break in. Well, not *break in*. Not really. We just wanted to see what the place looks like now. But every door was locked tight, every window shade drawn shut.

I pedal quickly down my street, cross Burton Boulevard after looking both ways, then coast down Ewing Street, where everything in town happens. The air always smells like salt here, but it's stronger now that I'm closer to the beach. I have to get off my bike after a while and walk it next to me because the sidewalk is too cluttered with tourists to ride. And the street is too cluttered with cars waiting for the tourists who spill out from the sidewalk to mosey along.

Coleman Creamery is in the perfect spot on Ewing Street, sandwiched between Rosa's Tacos and the surf shop. Three of my favorite places. I lock up my bike on the side of the building since all the racks out front are full. Once the summer's over, my bike will probably be the only one here.

Instead of a bell, the creamery makes a mooing sound when you walk in. I used to think it was funny when I was little. Dad or Elliott would let me push open the door, and I'd squeal each time as if it were my first visit. It's so embarrassing now to have a cow sound off every time you open the door. I keep my head down as I walk to the counter.

Laramie Mason is sitting on the stool in front of the cash register, legs swinging back and forth as she licks at her cookies-and-cream-filled waffle cone. I think her legs are at least three times longer than when we finished sixth grade, and that was only a couple of months ago. I don't understand how she's getting taller while everything about me is staying the same.

"Hey." I slide onto the seat next to her. The stools are the old-fashioned kind with red glitter vinyl seats that swivel around.

"Hey!" She bumps me with her shoulder. "I tried to wait for you, but he was almost out of cookies and cream and I was totally craving it today. I had to act fast."

"It's okay," I say, looking behind the counter.

Laramie's big brother, Leif, is scooping up ice cream. Laramie and her brother are the ones with hippie names, but she's always teasing me about my family being the real hippies. I guess because we don't eat meat, and we only use all-natural cleaning products and soap from local companies, and Dad has a compost bin in the backyard. And I don't think that makes us any more hippie than a lot of people in California, but...

Before I was born, Dad and Elliott lived on an artists commune. They lived and made art with dozens of other painters and sculptors and illustrators. Then Elliott went back to school so he could be a professor, and Dad decided to open an art gallery. The commune is where they met. It's also where they met my surrogate mother, Denise.

Leif rings up some customers and checks to make sure no one else is waiting. Then he walks over to me with a smile that shows off his perfect white teeth. Laramie complains that everybody thinks Leif is so cute, but it's a fact. He's sixteen, and he looks like what people think of when they think of California boys. He is tanned and has floppy golden hair and big, sparkling blue eyes.

"How's it going, Alberta?" He gives me a high five, even though I think I'm getting too old for high fives from him. Or maybe it's annoying because I don't think boys his age high-five girls they think are pretty. "What can I get for you?"

"It's going good. Can I get a scoop of butter pecan?"

"Got a new flavor in this week," Leif says. "Key lime pie. Want to try it?"

I shake my head. "No, thank you. Just the usual, please."

"Butter pecan in a sugar cone. Got it," he says, saluting me.

I've always liked Leif because he's a surfer, like me. He's on the Ewing Beach High surf team, and sometimes I'll go with Laramie and her mom to watch his contests. We don't have a surf team in middle school, but as soon as I get to high school in two years, I'm trying out.

Leif carefully hands me the cone with a small square napkin wrapped around the bottom. "On the house," he says. He always says that, even though he knows Laramie and I wouldn't be up here so often if the ice cream weren't free.

"Thank you." I smile at him. When he goes to the other end of the counter to help a customer, I turn to Laramie. "A new family is moving into the bed and breakfast."

"No way." She takes the first bite of her waffle

cone with a hearty crunch. "Someone's finally moving into the Harris Inn?"

"Yeah, and my dad says they have a daughter our age. They just moved in today. Finally, we'll have someone our age on my street."

"Well, technically, you have Nicolette."

"Nicolette is the worst person I know."

Laramie laughs. "Come on, Alberta. The worst?"

I stare at her. "Give me one good reason I should like Nicolette McKee."

"I don't know. She was just up here, with her brother and nanny. I saw them outside and she said hey."

"So just because she said hi to you, she's nice?"

Laramie sighs. "I didn't say that. I just... She's not the worst person I know."

Ugh. I hate when Laramie gets like this. Like she's forgotten all the terrible things Nicolette has said to me over the years. I wouldn't forget if someone had said those things to her.

"Well, the new neighbors are black," I say, getting back to what we're supposed to be talking about. I don't want to think about Nicolette.

"Nice," Laramie says.

Nice? I take a bite of butter pecan and roll the cool cream around in my mouth until it melts on my tongue. I feel like she should be saying more than *nice*, but I guess I don't know exactly what I want her to say.

"I think it's *really* nice. There definitely aren't any black people on my street. There are barely any at school."

"What about Rashawn? And Noah?" Laramie says. She's counting them off on her fingers, which makes me feel weird.

"You forgot about Deanna," I say after a few moments.

"Oh. Right. And she's going into ninth grade."

"Exactly. She doesn't even go to our school anymore. Even if she was there, four people isn't a lot. I'm the only black kid in our grade."

Laramie looks down at her cone, nodding slowly. "I guess I never thought about it. You're just *you*. You're Alberta. You blend in. I don't really think about you being black."

I get that same tight feeling in my stomach, like when she was counting names on her fingers. I want to say that yes, I am Alberta, but part of being Alberta is being black. And I *don't* blend in here in Ewing Beach.

That is something else I know for a fact.

But Laramie is my best friend. I don't think she meant anything by it, and I don't want to start a fight. She's been kind of mopey lately.

I change the subject. I ask her what she's wearing on the first day of school so I won't accidentally say something that makes me sound as annoyed as I am.

SKINFOLK

WHEN I GET HOME, ELLIOTT IS SITTING ON THE couch with his legs stretched long in front of him. His eyes are closed.

"Hey, Al," he says when the front door clicks shut. He doesn't open his eyes.

I sink down next to him. "What if I was someone breaking into the house?"

"First of all, the crime rate in Ewing Beach doesn't support that theory." He leans over to kiss me hello. Eyes still closed. "Second, if you were breaking in, you'd quickly find we have nothing worth taking except all that gorgeous artwork. And third, our taste is too abstract for your typical burglar." He collapses against the couch cushions and sighs as if that explanation exhausted him. "Where ya been?"

"Ice cream and then the surf shop with Laramie." I think she only suggested the surf shop after our weird conversation in the creamery. We didn't talk about it anymore, but I'm pretty sure she could tell it was bugging me.

"Sounds like a nice afternoon." He opens one eye to peer at me. "Want to know what I did today?"

"Yes, please." I slide off my flip-flops and bring my knees up to my chin.

"Well, I had a discussion with a student that got rather...heated." Both his eyes are open now. He sighs. "I appreciate the passion, but it's a bit early in the semester for all that."

"What were you so heated about?"

"Kehinde Wiley." Elliott's mouth quirks up in a wry smile. "Let's just say only one of us recognizes the man's brilliance. How was the last day of surf camp?"

"Fine." I pause because I feel Elliott's eyes on me.

He looks at me long and hard, the way he always does when he knows I'm not being truthful. "It *was* fine, but I hate that it's over."

Anything feels possible when I'm in the ocean, paddling out to catch a wave. I've felt that way ever since my first surfing lesson. I can't wait to compete, but even if I wasn't that good, I think I'd still love it.

"There's always next summer," Elliott says. "And the one after that, and the one after that…"

"Or there's still time for me to enter the contest at the festival in Pismo Beach…."

Elliott shakes his head. "Are you having a birthday between now and then that I don't know about?"

"But I'll be thirteen six months after the contest. Can't you make an exception?"

"Al, I know you'd live in the ocean if you could, but a rule is a rule. Six months will be here before you know it."

I frown. So will the contest they won't let me compete in.

"Well…" I pause as if Nicolette will jump out from behind the couch to question what I'm saying. "Irene said I was the best surfer in camp."

Elliott gives me a fist bump. "I always knew I liked Irene. Great job, Al."

"Great enough to enter the contest?"

"You can still go surfing, even if camp is over," he says. "Just no competing. We could head down to the beach on Sunday, if you want. Kick off the school year right and all that."

I shrug, even though I really just want to stomp off and pout about the fact that I have to wait a whole year to start competing. But I'm pretty sure that won't convince him I'm mature enough. "Maybe. I'm going down on Saturday for the camp party with Laramie."

He nudges my shoulder with his. "All right. How about some pizza to celebrate you being the best?"

I give Elliott a grudging smile, but it turns into a real one after a few seconds. He may not get why I want to compete so badly, but he *does* get why it's important that I'm one of the best surfers in Ewing Beach.

The pizza comes just before Dad gets home. When I'm cleaning up after dinner, my eyes land on the glass cake stand sitting a few feet down. It's empty now, but we go to Ewing Street Bakery on the weekends and fill it with all kinds of pastries and doughnuts.

That gives me an idea.

"What if we bring the new neighbors something?"

Dad and Elliott look up from the table where they're reading on Dad's phone. Elliott's eyebrows are scrunched together behind his glasses.

"Like what?" he asks.

"Like a cake…or a pie…or…I don't know. Something that says welcome to the neighborhood."

"Yeah, sure," he says, nodding. "I can pick up something after work tomorrow at the bakery. What about cookies?"

I wrinkle my nose. "Store-bought cookies aren't very special."

"What about bakery-bought?"

I shake my head.

Elliott laughs. "Since when? You don't seem to have a problem with them any other time."

"I know, but…what if we made something instead?" My eyes slide to Dad.

Because the truth is, I've never made a cake or a pie or…anything, really. Elliott knows that. And he's no help in the kitchen except making sure we keep it organized and sparkling clean. Dad is my only hope here.

He looks at me, scratching under his chin like he's thinking. His eyes sweep around the kitchen, landing on the bunch of bananas sitting on the counter. We got them at the farmers market last Saturday, but nobody has eaten any yet. They're spotted with brown marks that are starting to turn black.

"How about banana bread?" he suggests.

"Good idea, Kadeem," Elliott says. "Who doesn't like banana bread?"

I nod my approval, too. Mostly because I don't know how to make anything, but I *do* like banana bread. I'd be happy if a new neighbor brought us some.

"Sounds like a plan," Dad says, but he's distracted. He's already staring back down at his phone again. I wonder what they're looking at. They don't really like us using our phones at the table, even after we've eaten.

"Can we bake it tonight?" I prod him. Suddenly all I can think about is making banana bread. Or *learning* how to make it.

"Sure, as long as the kitchen is cleaned up before bed."

Elliott looks pleased.

"Deal," I say.

I only have a few more days to sleep in until school starts, but I get up early the next morning to have breakfast with my dads. Today's the day we're meeting the new neighbors.

Dad doesn't go into the gallery until later. Usually not until it's been open at least a couple of hours. He has people to take care of things, so sometimes he doesn't show up until after lunch. But he always gets up early to have breakfast with Elliott before Elliott drives to San Luis Obispo for work. It's about twenty minutes up the Central Coast from Ewing Beach.

"Well, you're up early," Dad says, running a hand over the top of my dreadlocks.

I've already poured a bowl of cereal and almond milk. Elliott is making coffee in the French press, wearing his professor clothes: a dark button-down shirt, dress shoes, and khaki pants. I couldn't believe it when I first saw pictures of him and Dad from the commune. There's one of Elliott standing in a field wearing a pair of bright red overalls with a black plastic rose in the front pocket.

"Don't you think we should go meet the neighbors this morning? They might be busy in the afternoon." I shovel a spoonful of Cheerios into my mouth.

Dad peers at the banana bread. We wrapped it up in plastic last night after it cooled. "Mmm-mmm-mmm, this sure would be good with a cup of coffee," he says.

"Dad."

"I kid, Alberta. But we'll wrap it up nice for them before we take it over. Make it look like more of a gift."

I don't know how he's planning to do that, but Dad is good at making things look fancy and nice, so I just nod.

Elliott sits down with a plate of avocado toast. "You two seem awfully invested in these new neighbors. Do you know something about them that I don't? Are they superheroes? A family of mind readers?"

"They're black," I say. And I think that should

be enough of an explanation, but Elliott still looks confused.

"Just because they're black doesn't mean they're going to be our new best friends," he says slowly. "We don't know anything about them."

"But..." I don't want to have another weird conversation about being black. Not that it would be the same as when I was talking to Laramie, but sometimes Elliott and Dad disagree when they talk about race. I always feel like I have to choose sides, even though I thought we were all on the same team.

"Go on, Al," Elliott encourages.

"Well, when we go to parties and bonfires, you and Dad always go up to the black people first. Sometimes you spend almost the whole night talking to them. Or if you see black people you don't even know when we're downtown, you nod at them. Like you're already friends. Isn't this sort of like that?"

"Huh." Elliott drinks his coffee. "I see what you mean. But I don't want you putting expectations on people. We might have more in common with, say, the McKees than the new neighbors."

I make a face into my cereal. Bad example. We have absolutely nothing in common with the McKees and Elliott knows it.

Dad comes up behind him and slides a hand onto his shoulder. "I think what your dear father is trying to say is that all our skinfolk ain't kinfolk."

"What?"

Elliott's hand reaches up to meet Dad's and squeezes. "Yes, exactly. Just because we're black and the new neighbors are black doesn't mean we have the same values or interests."

"*But,*" Dad adds, "it's always a good idea to reach out to your skinfolk. Especially when they're new in the community. And *especially* when there are barely any of us here in the first place."

Elliott frowns a little. "Well, there are more of us now than there ever have been. It could always be worse."

"All of us combined are less than 0.5 percent of the population," Dad says, looking at him. "We can still count the number of families on two hands. Yes, it could be worse, but not much."

Dad and Elliott don't look angry when they argue.

They never raise their voices—at least not around me—but they don't hide that they're disagreeing. "Nothing wrong with a little healthy discourse," Elliott always says, and Dad always says that just means he likes to argue. But he usually smiles or hugs him or kisses him by his ear when he says that. And Elliott always smiles and hugs and kisses him back.

"Okay, okay." Elliott holds up his hands like he's been defeated. "I expect a full report on our new best friends at dinner tonight."

I slurp up the last of my cereal. After I rinse and put my bowl in the dishwasher, Dad pours more coffee in his mug and says, "Want to help me wrap up this loaf?"

We carefully unpeel the plastic and set the bread on a piece of waxed paper. My father trims one end of the paper with kitchen shears, making a sharp, straight line the whole way down. Then I help him neatly fold the sides over, and we wrap the loaf in another sheet of waxed paper and tie it with a piece of twine from the spool in the kitchen junk drawer.

"Perfect," he says, admiring our work.

It does look really good. I hope the new neighbors like it.

I know Elliott doesn't want me to get too excited, but I hope the new neighbors are kinfolk.

3

PURE BLACK

D<small>AD AND</small> I <small>WAIT UNTIL TEN</small> <small>O</small>'<small>CLOCK</small> ("A <small>RESPECT-</small> able time for a visit," he says) before we head over to the B&B.

I wear my white cutoffs and my favorite pink tank top, but I am still nervous. What if Elliott is right? What if we have nothing in common with them? What if the new girl is *worse* than Nicolette McKee?

Dad rings the bell to the inn. I'm clutching the bread in a death grip so it won't slip out of my nervous hands. We don't hear anything from inside. Maybe they left the car and went on a walk? I didn't see anyone come out.

He looks at me, shrugs, and rings the bell again. "We can leave it on the porch with a note if they aren't home," he says.

I try to look like I'm okay with this plan, but I feel deflated at the thought. After all that time making the bread and picking out the perfect outfit and waiting for this very moment, I don't want to leave without meeting them.

But then there are footsteps. And the lace curtains rustle in the window next to the door. My skin tingles when I hear the lock click.

A tall woman with dark brown skin and pretty eyes opens the door. She looks surprised to see us, then smiles. "Good morning. We're not open for business yet, but—"

"Oh, we're your neighbors," Dad says quickly, smiling back. "I'm Kadeem Freeman-Price, and this is my daughter, Alberta. We live across the street."

"The blue house," I say.

"Oh." The woman's eyebrows are raised so high I wonder if they're going to shoot off her face. "Wow. Well, hello."

"Sorry to drop by like this," my dad says. "We know you need to get settled. We just wanted to say welcome to the neighborhood and drop off some banana bread. Alberta and I baked it."

"We did," I say, holding it out.

"You baked this? For us?" The woman still looks so shocked, even as she takes the bread from my hands. "That is so kind of you. I—oh, excuse me. I haven't introduced myself. I'm Calliope Whitman."

"Nice to meet you," Dad says, shaking her free hand.

"We just flew in yesterday and I'm so frazzled and"—she lowers her voice as if the whole town is listening—"well, to be honest, I wasn't expecting to see any of *us* for a while. Especially not living on my own street."

My father laughs. "We know the feeling, trust me. We live with Alberta's other father, my husband, Elliott. The three of us have been the only black people on this street for the decade we've lived here. We're happy to see you, too."

Ms. Whitman laughs, and I like it right away. It is deep and warm, and she shows a lot of teeth. "Would you like to come in? Our things haven't arrived yet, but we have coffee and fruit if you'd like some."

Dad looks at me sideways. "You know what goes good with coffee?"

Ms. Whitman taps the banana bread in her hand. "It definitely does. Please, if you have time, come in. Alberta, I want you to meet my daughter, Edie. You look about her age."

"I'm twelve," I say. "I'll be in seventh grade."

"Edie is twelve, exactly! Oh, I can't believe how well this is already working out." She holds the door wider for us to come in. Then Ms. Whitman stands at the bottom of the stairs and calls up, "Edie! Come down here, please. We have company."

Dad closes the front door, and Ms. Whitman leads us to the kitchen. She's asking my father what he does. I'm glad she's not asking me questions, because I'm too busy gazing around the B&B. It looks familiar, but it's been a long time since I was in here. Not since Mrs. Harris had her last holiday party, and I think I was in fourth grade then.

"An art gallery?" Ms. Whitman shakes her head with a smile. "That's so wonderful. And I hope you won't judge me, because we haven't had a chance to put our own touch on the B&B just yet. The sale included the furniture."

Dad looks around. "Mrs. Harris was old-fashioned, but they spruced up the place quite a bit after she…" He clears his throat. I wonder if Ms. Whitman knows why the B&B was for sale. "Maybe just look into some new linens and a reupholstery or two and you'll be good to go."

"I'm sure you're busy, but I'd be forever grateful if you could help us pick out some art for the walls sometime?" She sighs. "Decorating is not my forte."

"I'd be happy to," Dad says. "Elliott also has a real eye. He teaches studio art and art history at Cal Poly."

I keep listening for footsteps on the stairs, but I don't hear anything. Ms. Whitman must notice the silence at the same time because she pokes her head around the corner and calls out again. "Edie, please come down here now. Our new neighbors are here."

I keep picturing different versions of the girl upstairs. One version is wearing cornrows. Another one has a big smile with braces and an Afro puff. And another one looks a little like me, but without the straight-up-and-down little-girl body.

Ms. Whitman pulls a butter knife from a drawer and examines it closely. "Full disclosure, I forgot to pick up dish soap *and* new silverware yesterday, so we've been eating with these. They...came with the house."

That would bother Elliott *so much*, but Dad just shrugs. "Looks clean enough to me. What doesn't kill us, right?"

"Then I guess we'll keep taking our chances." She cuts into the banana bread.

Finally, I hear feet clomping down the stairs. My heart starts beating a little faster and I'm feeling the same kind of nervous as when we stepped onto the porch a few minutes ago. I try to guess which version of the girl will come in this room, but I can't decide. She could be anyone. And at the last second, I think she's probably not anything like I imagined.

Ms. Whitman looks up and smiles. "There she is. Edie, these are our new neighbors from across the street. Alberta and her father Kadeem."

I see Dad's face before I look at Edie. And it is... well, I don't know if *surprised* is the right word. Then I turn around and—I was right. I never would have guessed Edie looks like this.

She's tall, like her mom. And she is dressed all in black: a black tank top, a long black skirt, and black combat boots. Even her hair is long and straight and midnight black. But I can't stop staring at her face. At her *lips*. They are the darkest color I've ever seen: *pure black*. And it looks even darker because her skin is a light, light brown.

I can't believe she's allowed to wear makeup. I can't believe she's my age. I feel about eight years old next to her in my white and pink.

She gives me a small smile. "Hey, I'm Edie. I like your hair."

I touch my locs and smile. Suddenly I don't feel so nervous.

Edie and her mother are from New York City.

"I've never been there," I say.

Edie sighs. "I miss Brooklyn already. I miss *every-thing* about it. Our brownstone, our bodega, our cat."

I don't know what a brownstone is, but it seems like something I should know, so I don't ask. I don't even pretend to know the other word.

"What's a bodega?"

Edie's eyes light up. "You've never heard of a

bodega?" I'm starting to get used to her dark lipstick, but I still stare at her mouth when she talks. I can't help it. Even Laramie doesn't get to wear makeup yet.

I shake my head.

"It's, like...quintessential New York." She pauses. "Like a convenience store, sort of. You can buy everything there. Chips, laundry stuff, Band-Aids, phone chargers, hot food...everything! And they almost always have a cat."

"Wait," I say. "Your cat lives at the bodega?"

"No, my cat was *my* cat. Arnold. But lots of cats live in bodegas."

"Oh, like Jordan," I say. "The tortie who lives at the library."

She nods. "Everything was sort of dusty in our bodega. But I loved going there. They knew me and my family. And I miss their egg and cheeses. We didn't have time to get one yesterday before we went to the airport, so I don't even know when I'll have one again."

We're upstairs in her bedroom, which spreads across the entire top floor. The attic.

I look around. It's a little musty up here, but even

under the layers of dust, I can see it's a great room. Thick wooden beams drop down from the ceiling, and there's a small window shaped like a hexagon. A couple of boxes are shoved in the corner, but they look like they were here before Edie and her mom. There's a bed with an iron frame, and a bookshelf across the room.

"I can't believe your mom is letting you sleep up here. It's so cool."

I remember that Mrs. Harris's room and another bedroom are on the bottom floor. The guest rooms are on the second level, the one under us.

"Yeah. She feels guilty about splitting up with my dad, so she's being extra nice right now." Edie shrugs.

"You won't be scared sleeping up here?"

"Are you kidding? I can't wait till my stuff comes, but the bed was already here, and I love it. This is the best room ever. It's like I live in a Victorian novel." She pauses. "Do you like the Brontë sisters?"

"Um...I don't know?"

"They were writers. They wrote some of the best books ever. Like *Jane Eyre* and *Wuthering Heights*."

"I thought those were movies."

"They started out as books," she says, giving me a look like she doesn't know if she should forgive me for not knowing that.

"Oh. Well, I'm sort of more into movies."

She perks up at this. "I like movies, too. What kind are you into?"

"Horror, mostly."

"Really?" She stares at me like we rewound to fifteen minutes ago and she's just seeing me for the first time.

"What?"

"Well, no offense, but you don't really seem like someone who'd like horror."

My mouth drops open. "You just met me!"

"I know, but you look so...innocent." Her eyes roam over my pink top. Not in a judgy way, but it still makes me shrink, hugging my knees to my flat chest.

"Do *you* like horror?"

She makes a face. "Why? Because I'm wearing all black?"

I shrug. "Well...yeah."

"Horror and gothic aren't the same things."

"Oh."

"But I like some horror movies. And I *love* Halloween, because everyone feels free to dress exactly how they want to."

"Dad, Elliott, and I have a horror movie marathon every Halloween," I say. "You should come over this year."

Laramie tried to watch with us exactly one time before she said never again to our movie marathon. When she got home, she had to leave all the lights on to go to sleep, and when that didn't work, she convinced Leif to let her sleep on his bedroom floor. *Jaws* was the one that got her. To be fair, even I stayed out of the water for a few weeks after that one.

"Do you dress up, too? I can't wait till Halloween this year. I'm going to—oh." Her big brown eyes drop to her lap.

"What's wrong?"

"Nothing," Edie mumbles.

It's obviously something. "What did you do when you lived in New York?"

"That's the thing," she says, looking up at me through her curtain of hair. "I forgot I'm not going to be there for it this year. My dad's friends always have a huge party, but tons of kids our age go, too. And there's a big costume contest. I won best prize last year."

"What were you?"

She smiles now. "Coraline. My mom played the Other Mother and put buttons over her eyes."

"That sounds really cool." *Coraline* is one of my favorites, too.

"It was. Everyone loved it." She sighs. "And now I'm stuck here. No offense," she quickly adds.

I shrug like I don't care, even though I don't like what she said. What's so bad about Ewing Beach? "Actually, a lot of people go up to SLO for Halloween."

"What's SLO?"

"San Luis Obispo," I say.

"Oh, that's where my mom and I flew in!"

"They have a haunted cave and show scary movies and have costume parties, too."

Edie sits up a little. "A haunted cave?"

"Mm-hmm."

"Do you ever go?"

"Sometimes. Maybe my dads can take us this year."

Edie smiles, her eyes drifting down to my neck. "What's that?"

I finger the silver necklace I wear every day. Dad and Elliott gave it to me for my last birthday. "A surfboard."

Her eyes widen. "You *surf*?"

"It's my favorite thing in the world. Do you?"

"Oh my god, no!" She shakes her head back and forth so fast it makes me dizzy. "I can't even swim."

I stare at her. "Are you serious? What do you do at the beach?"

Edie blinks back at me. "I don't go to the beach. Not unless it's Coney Island."

"What's so special about Coney Island?"

"Alberta, you need a lesson on New York City, stat," she says in a bossy voice. But she says it with a smile.

"And I can tell you all about the Central Coast," I say. "Deal?"

"Deal," she says, and we shake on it.

Well, I guess we can't have *everything* in common. Laramie and I don't.

Besides, no matter what Elliott said about skin-folk versus kinfolk, it seems more important to think about what Edie and I *do* have in common. Which is something I don't share with many people in this town—and I think that has to count for something.

FEMININE PERSPECTIVE

DAD CALLS A FAMILY MEETING AFTER DINNER.

Our last one was a year ago, when we talked about getting a pet. I wanted a dog. I didn't care what kind. Just whichever one I liked best at the shelter. I even had a name picked out: I would call her Gidget after the surfer my dads showed me in this really old TV show, and she'd come down to the beach with me and chase the tide. Elliott wanted a cat because he said they're clean and quiet. Dad was our tiebreaker—he didn't want anything.

The meeting before that one was about Elliott's job. Another college wanted to hire him, but it was all the way across the country, in Maine. Elliott said we'd just be moving from one beach community to another, but I could tell his heart wasn't in it. He didn't take the job. And even though Dad and I both said we'd move without a fuss if it made him happy, I was glad he didn't.

I try to guess what the meeting is about during dinner, but they won't tell me. They don't look mad, though, so I'm not in trouble. At least I hope not.

Family meetings are held in our tiny backyard at the picnic table under the paper lanterns. It's cool at nighttime in Ewing Beach, even in the summer. So Elliott makes chai and we take it outside where we bundle into beach blankets under the stars.

"Why do we always have our meetings outside?" I asked Dad once.

He breathed in deeply and looked at me. "There's something about the fresh air that makes people think more clearly," he said, letting out his breath slowly.

Tonight is extra chilly. I wrap the woolly red-and-black plaid blanket around me as tight as it will go and watch the steam curl up from our mugs.

"I officially call this meeting of the Freeman-Price

family to order," Dad says in a voice that he thinks makes him sound businesslike. I think he sounds more like the ringmaster of a circus: too loud and a little bit silly.

Elliott smiles and pounds his fist on the table like a gavel.

I try not to roll my eyes.

Dad looks at me. "We have some news, Alberta."

Oh no. Are we moving to Maine after all? Or am I going to have to do something I hate, like the time I had to take ballet lessons to make sure I have a "well-rounded childhood"? The leotard was so tight I wanted to tear it right off. My wet suits are even tighter, but those are different. They keep me warm when the water is freezing. I was cold every single time I wore that leotard. And I wasn't interested in pointing my toes or moving my arms like a swan.

"*Good* news," Elliott says from across the table.

I look back and forth from him to Dad. "What is it?"

"You know Denise," Dad says slowly.

Of course I know Denise. She's my surrogate mother. The doctor implanted her with Elliott's sperm to make a baby. Which ended up being me.

"And you know she's getting ready to have a baby herself," he goes on.

I nod. She had just gotten pregnant the last time she came to visit, at the beginning of the year, but you couldn't tell yet.

"Well, it turns out that Tim has to go away for work. They didn't plan it, of course, and it can't be avoided. He'll be gone a few weeks, right up until the baby is about to be born."

"So," Elliott takes over, "we thought she'd come stay with us for the last few weeks of her pregnancy. She can get away from the bustle of L.A. and spend some time here in Ewing Beach."

"How does that sound?" Dad asks.

"Sounds good to me."

I like Denise, but it's almost impossible to not like Denise. She's a sunny person, always smiling and laughing and sweet. She gives the best hugs, her hair always looks pretty, and she smells like patchouli and oranges.

We see her a couple of times a year, usually when she and her husband are passing through on their way to San Francisco. They came up for Dad's fiftieth birthday party last year, and we stayed at her and

Tim's house when we went to L.A. for a big art show when I was ten.

"We thought it might be nice for you to have her around," Elliot says. "Another...feminine perspective. But we wanted to be sure it's all right with you, too, since she's going to be sharing space with all of us." He's giving me that serious look. The one that says I'd better not lie.

"It's all right with me." I pause. "But what is she going to do while she's here?"

I get annoyed when people who don't live here say Ewing Beach is boring, but the truth is you can do pretty much everything in town in two days. And there's even less to do after Labor Day, when half the restaurants shut down for the season and all the other businesses cut their hours.

"Well, she's a journalist—freelance, so she can work from anywhere," says Dad. "But the idea is that she'll get a lot of rest while she's waiting for the baby."

I've never been around anyone who's pregnant. Will she have strange food cravings? What if the baby comes early, while Tim is still away?

"What's she having?" I take a careful sip of my

chai, hoping it's not still too hot. It's perfect, though, and it goes down milky, spicy smooth.

"They're waiting to find out," Dad answers. "Denise says it's one of life's only true surprises. They're so excited. You know, I think Denise was a bit sad that she couldn't keep you when you were born."

"What?"

"Kadeem." Elliott says it lightly, but it still sounds like a warning.

Dad waves a hand at him. "Oh, she's old enough. Besides, what's so bad about hearing you were so loved that someone wanted to be your mother?"

"Is that true?" I ask slowly. "Denise wanted to keep me?"

"She never said so. But we were in the room with her, and the way she looked at you—"

"She'd just given birth," Elliott interrupts him. "It's a huge life event. There are a lot of hormones and emotions involved."

Dad sighs. "You're right. I shouldn't speak for Denise." He turns to me. "But she does care about you very much."

"Yes," Elliott says, his voice softer. "Ever since you were just a twinkle in our eyes."

I look down at the table. I never know what to say when they talk about me before I remember being me. Most of my friends don't seem to think too much about how they came into the world. It's like they just knew they would exist, no matter what. But I know how badly my dads wanted me and how it wasn't as easy for them as just deciding they were going to have a baby.

"When will Denise get here?" I ask.

"Well, since you've given the okay, we'll call her tonight and find out," Dad says. "Tim has to get on the road pretty soon, so maybe as early as next week."

Next week? That's so soon. I'm starting seventh grade next week, and Edie just moved in, and for some reason it seems like so many big things shouldn't be happening so close together.

I head to Laramie's the next day after I eat lunch with Dad. I used to go over for lunch sometimes, until Dad figured out Leif was making things like chicken nuggets and fried bologna sandwiches. We're vegetarians, so sometimes all I could eat were frozen french fries or ice cream from one of the pints Leif brings home from the creamery. (Even though, to be honest, some of the meat smelled *really* good.) Dad freaked out and said I couldn't eat over there until they started serving real food. I haven't had a meal at Laramie's since.

Today, she and I can't decide what to do.

"We could go to the beach," I say. It's usually my first idea, and it's only a few steps out Laramie's back door.

We're sitting on the floor of her bedroom in the middle of the rug. She stretches her legs in front of her and I try not to notice how much they've grown.

Laramie makes a face as she wiggles her bare toes. "I don't feel like dealing with the sand today."

Which is ridiculous because you can't walk through Laramie's house barefoot without getting sand between your toes. It comes with the territory.

"What about the comic shop?" It only seems fair to suggest it since she went to the surf shop with me the other day.

Laramie picks at a loose thread on the rug. "The new comics don't come out until next Wednesday."

"Oh." I knew that. "The creamery?" Leif's working again.

She shakes her head, still looking down.

"What *do* you want to do?"

"I don't know. Nothing sounds good. I'm almost excited school is starting next week."

I stare at her. "What's wrong?"

"Nothing."

"Laramie."

She sighs and looks at me as she unties her curly blond hair from its ponytail and loops the elastic tie around her wrist. "I started. Last night."

I frown. "Started what?"

She stares at me, her brown eyes serious. "Come on, Alberta. Think about it."

I do, and then my face gets hot. "Your period?" I whisper it even though we're here alone. Laramie seems embarrassed, and it makes me feel embarrassed, too.

"Yeah," she says softly. "It's weird. My mom was all proud, like I had something to do with it. I just wish..."

"What?"

"I wish things weren't changing so much. That *I* wasn't changing so much. Mom measured me last night, and I've grown almost three inches this *summer*. I feel awkward all the time and—it's just happening too fast. Everything."

"Sorry." I twist my hands together. I'm not sure what to say. I know what she means about things changing too fast, but my body definitely isn't on that list. I feel bad for being jealous of her, but I am. Maybe I would feel the same way Laramie does if I were the one who'd started first... but I don't think so.

"It is what it is." Laramie sounds so grown-up when she says that, but she looks scared and small. She snaps the hair elastic against her wrist. "Do I get to meet the new girl before school starts?"

I told her all about Edie after Dad and I got back from the B&B. Laramie sounded interested when I said that Edie is obsessed with horror movies and came from Brooklyn, but in a way that I think means she's only interested because I am. Laramie is popular. She doesn't really need new friends. We hang out with the same people, so I guess I don't need a new friend, either. But I don't have any black friends. Not ones that I actually see outside of school.

"What about Saturday? Do you care if she comes with us to the surf camp party?"

"Cool with me," Laramie says.

She looks slightly less miserable than she did five minutes ago, so I try one more time. With something we both love to do together. "Want to see what the thrift store got in this week?"

Laramie's face finally brightens.

5

BIOLOGICAL

EDIE AND MS. WHITMAN COME OVER FOR DINNER ON Friday night.

Dad and Elliott are stumbling over each other in the kitchen, trying to make everything perfect. When the doorbell rings, they don't even stop talking, like they didn't hear it. I go to the door without being asked.

Ms. Whitman is holding a pie plate covered in foil. She air-kisses me on both cheeks. I always think it looks fake when people do that in movies and on TV, but I don't mind it from her. Everything about Edie's mom seems genuine.

"I hope you all like blueberry pie," she says,

handing me the plate. "I went a little wild with the berries at the farmers market this morning."

"We love it. Thank you," I say just as my fathers come out of the kitchen.

Dad is wearing a KISS THE COOK apron and Elliott has on his professor clothes, even though he had plenty of time to change after work. Is he trying to impress the new neighbors, too? This is the first time they've met, and I notice his smile is extra big as he shakes Ms. Whitman's hand, just like when we see other black people downtown.

I take the pie into the kitchen and when I come back out, Elliott is asking Ms. Whitman if she wants a drink before dinner. I look at Edie, who has on fresh black lipstick and a gauzy black dress that goes all the way down to her ankles. The toes of her boots peek out from under the hem. I'm wearing a sky-blue romper printed with orange butterflies. It's one of my favorite outfits, but next to Edie, I feel like a baby. I think maybe I'll never feel cool standing next to her.

"Want to see my room?" I ask. Even though I know it isn't her style. I'm all bright colors and patterns, and I can't imagine Edie wearing any color besides black.

She nods and follows me down the hallway.

My bedroom has white furniture and a butter-yellow duvet on a bed with a nest of pillows. Every wall is covered with artwork except the one that butts up against my bed. That one is painted white and dotted with pale and dark blue spots of all different sizes that look like watercolor. It reminds me of the ocean. But the best part of my room is the big bay window that lets in tons of light—and the long, comfy window seat underneath.

Edie walks over to it and plops right down on the blue cushion. It matches my watercolor wall. "I've always wanted a window seat."

"It's my favorite thing," I say. "I love to sit there and..."

She looks at me. "What?"

I shrug, suddenly feeling silly. But I go on because even though Edie and I aren't very similar at all, she feels like someone I can trust not to make fun of me for being myself.

"Sometimes I like to sit there and look at the stars and just...think."

"What do you think about?" she asks, staring out the window as if it will give away my secrets.

"Just...stuff." Like why I can't ignore the things Nicolette says about me. Or, lately, why all the girls I know seem to only be interested in talking about boys and how cute they are. I think some of them are cute, too, but having a boyfriend seems so...grown-up. And I know Dad and Elliott would say I'm too young to have one, anyway.

Edie nods like she understands exactly, and maybe that's why I trust her. We barely know each other, but she doesn't make me explain myself too much. Especially when I don't even know how to say it.

Laughter breaks out in the living room, interrupting my thoughts.

"Why do you call him Elliott?" Edie asks, tilting her head toward the front of the house. "I thought you said he was your dad, too?"

"Oh." Most people in Ewing Beach have known us so long that I don't have to explain anything about how the Freeman-Price family works. "He's my dad. They both are. We had a surrogate who gave them the egg, and they used Elliott's sperm."

"So he's your *real* dad," she says, pondering.

I frown. "Well, they're both my real dad. They've

been together forever. But Elliott is...biological. He didn't like any of the other names, like Daddy or Papa, and we thought it might be confusing if I called them both Dad. So he's always been Elliott."

She opens her mouth again and I *really* hope she isn't going to ask more questions. Our family is a lot for some people. Even people who don't have a problem with nontraditional families have *so many questions*. It seems like some of them wouldn't ever stop asking if we didn't change the subject first. I've watched Dad and Elliott talk to other adults about it, and by the end of the conversation, they always look like I feel: a little frustrated and completely exhausted.

But all Edie says is "He's cute."

My mouth is gaping. *"Elliott?"*

"Yeah, he's totally cute. I like his glasses," she says, then giggles.

I make a face and Edie laughs more. "What's your dad like?" I ask.

She turns on the seat so she's facing me completely, her back to the window. "The coolest person I know."

"Your dad?" I finally sit on my bed. For some

reason it takes me a while to relax when new people are in my room. Which doesn't happen very often. It's usually only Laramie, which is maybe why I notice how different I feel with Edie here.

"Yeah, he's a music producer. He works with a lot of hip-hop artists."

"Anyone I know?" I ask, even though I'm not really allowed to listen to hip-hop. Not the kind with swear words, which is usually the best kind. Dad caught me listening to it once, turned it off right away, and threatened to take away my internet if it happened again.

"*Everyone* you know." She plants her elbows on her knees and leans forward. "He's constantly hanging out with famous people. And he's won two Grammys."

I think it would seem like anyone else was bragging, but I can tell Edie is just really proud of her dad. And that she misses him.

"When do you get to see him again?"

She shrugs and tucks her hair behind her ears on both sides. The sleeves of her dress are puffy and sheer. It looks like a dress ladies would wear back in super-old Victorian times. "I don't know. Mom says we need to get settled here before I go back to New York."

"Maybe she'll let you fly back for Halloween?"

Edie shakes her head. "No, she doesn't want me missing school. We'll go back for winter break, and my dad and brother are coming out here for Thanksgiving."

"You have a brother?" This is the first time she's mentioned him. I thought she was an only child like me.

"Yeah, Craig. He's sixteen. He goes to Hunter College High School, so they didn't want to move him."

"Is that a good school?"

"It's really hard to get into. Craig and all his friends are *gifted*." She rolls her eyes. "So he got to stay."

"Why didn't you get to stay, too?" I blurt it out before I think about what I'm saying. My neck flushes hot when I realize it's kind of a rude question. The kind that my dads would be disappointed in me for asking, because it's too private. But I'm glad they're not sitting here because I'm not sorry I asked. I want to know.

"It's...complicated. My parents are pretty mad at each other." She lowers her voice. "I've heard my mom talking to her friends about how it's been a hard divorce. I think she left New York just to get away from my dad."

"Wow, really?"

Edie nods.

"What about your brother? Wasn't she sad to leave him?"

"Of course. But like I said, it's complicated. He's mad at her, even though I think the divorce is sort of my dad's fault. Craig said some really mean things to our mom. And I didn't want to make things worse for her and ask if I could stay in New York. Plus... I don't know. I kept thinking about her moving out here all by herself and it made me sort of sad."

I feel bad for Edie. I know from Laramie how hard it is just having one parent around. And Ms. Whitman seems great, but I don't think one great parent can make up for living thousands of miles away from the other one.

"It's okay," Edie says, looking at me now. I can't read her eyes to see if she really does think it's okay. But her voice is clearer. Stronger all of a sudden. "It'll be fine. My dad has to go to L.A. for work all the time, and he said he'll come visit. That's super close to here, right?"

"I think it's, like, three or four hours away." Which doesn't seem super close to me. I get antsy if we have to drive any farther than San Luis Obispo.

"That's closer than being all the way across the country."

"And he'd probably fly up here from L.A. anyway," I say, because it's a thought that just popped into my head, and it seems like a thing I should say to Edie right now.

"Yeah, you're right. He hates being in the car. He'd totally fly." She nods at me as if the matter has been settled. "It'll be fine."

But that's the second time she's said that in thirty seconds, and I wonder if she's still trying to convince herself that it's true.

"I hope a vegetarian meal is all right with you and Edie," Dad says easily to Ms. Whitman as he and Elliott take turns bringing food to the table. He carefully sets a spinach soufflé in the middle.

"Oh my goodness." Edie's mom claps her hands together. "It's so beautiful. You made this?"

"Yes, but trust me, it didn't look like this the first time I tried it." Dad smiles at her as he heads back to the dining room, passing Elliott, who's carrying a mushroom tart.

Ms. Whitman gazes admiringly at the table. "Everything looks so delicious. Are you all full-time vegetarians?"

"Kadeem and I have been for the past sixteen years, and Al has been her whole life," Elliott responds. "But we eat eggs and plenty of cheese, so we're not vegan."

"Well, I've been thinking about moving toward a more plant-based diet. Wouldn't that be a nice change, Edie?" Ms. Whitman pats Edie's arm.

"I mean, I guess?" Edie eyes the food suspiciously. "I think I'd miss meat too much to give it up forever." She glances at me. "So you don't eat hamburgers?"

"Veggie burgers," I say, taking a drink of water. "I haven't ever eaten meat."

Edie's eyes widen, suddenly huge on her face. She looks at me like she's just glimpsed a purple unicorn.

"You've never had a rotisserie chicken? Or *fried* chicken?"

I shake my head.

"No brisket? No *bacon*?"

Don't they have vegetarians in Brooklyn?

"I've literally never eaten meat." I shrug. "I don't really miss it since I've never had it."

It's my automatic answer, but sometimes I wonder if it's still true. I don't like the idea of eating animals, but I am curious what all of those things taste like.

"We try not to buy too many fake meat products, but they're worlds better than when we first went vegetarian back at the commune," Dad says.

I look down at my plate. I'm not embarrassed when they talk about the artists commune, but it's like the family thing. Once the floodgates are open, people start asking so many questions it makes my head hurt. Sometimes I wish my dads would just lie and say they met online.

Ms. Whitman is absolutely delighted. "You two lived on a commune?" Her shining eyes go back and forth from Dad to Elliott, who have finished laying out the food and are sitting down now.

"An artists commune," Elliott says. "Down in Ojai."

"It's where we met." Dad cuts into the soufflé and passes it to Ms. Whitman. "About a million years ago."

"Did you live there, too, Alberta?" she asks, serving herself before she passes the soufflé to Edie.

"No, it was before I was born." I take a piece of the mushroom tart and send it around the other side of the table to Dad.

He pats my shoulder. "Yes, this was pre-Alberta. There were some children who lived there, but most people didn't stay long after they had kids. We moved up here after Elliott finished his graduate program, when Alberta was two."

We pause conversation while we fill our plates, and I try not to watch Edie. I don't want to think about her judging the food we eat or the fact that I've never eaten meat. Lots of people don't eat animals because of their religion. Why is it so weird that we do it to help the environment?

Ms. Whitman takes a bite of soufflé and moans. "And you can *cook*, too! Is there gruyère in here?"

"Nice palate," Dad says, smiling. "How is the B&B going?"

"Well, our things are finally supposed to arrive tomorrow. I know Edie and I are pretty tired of living out of suitcases."

"When are you looking to open for business?" Elliott takes a bite of spicy bean salad.

"We're going to take a little bit of time to get things in order since the busy season is winding down. But we hope to be up and running by October. After I get through all the paperwork and freshen up the furniture and rooms." She pauses. "We're thinking of just calling it the Whitman Inn. What do you think?"

"I think it's perfect," Dad says with a nod. "Keep it straightforward and simple."

Ms. Whitman takes a breath. "A lot of people back in Brooklyn think I'm going through a midlife crisis for wanting to move out here and run a bed and breakfast. But it's my lifelong dream. That I put on hold for many years. So with our circumstances... this seemed like the best possible time to try it."

"A lifelong dream sounds like a good enough

reason to me," Dad responds. "You'll never have to wonder 'what if.'"

"Exactly," Edie's mom says, looking pleased.

"You know, we got a lot of questions about moving up here, too," Dad continues. "Ojai isn't very diverse, but the commune was. We heard Ewing Beach was starting to attract more families of color, so we thought we'd be okay helping pioneer that. But once we got here, it felt like someone had put the brakes on it and didn't tell us. All those families of color who were supposed to be buying houses and having kids never showed up."

Ms. Whitman sighs. "That was a concern of mine. Moving Edie from a place like Brooklyn to here. It's going to be an adjustment. That's why I just can't believe our luck, to have moved in across the street from you all."

"We feel lucky, too," Dad says.

Elliott turns to Edie. "How do you like living in a bed and breakfast?"

I'm surprised to see her steadily eating the food, almost like she enjoys it. She pauses and makes eye contact with him. Her light skin blushes. "It's all right. I like that my bedroom is in the attic."

"And are you girls looking forward to starting school next week?" Dad asks.

"I'm glad to not be a sixth grader anymore," I say. Back at Ewing Beach Elementary, our teachers warned us that we'd have triple the workload and super-strict teachers when we started sixth grade at the middle school. It turns out they were exaggerating a lot, but it's no fun being the new kids in the building. People's voices change when they say *sixth graders*, the same snooty way we used to talk about the kindergartners back in elementary school.

"I'm glad to have a friend already," Edie says. I guess she knows that new-kid feeling, too.

Her eyes slide over to me. Nervous, like maybe she shouldn't have said anything.

I give her a smile and she quickly returns it.

After dinner, Edie and I take our slices of blueberry pie out to the front porch (but only after Dad confirmed there was no lard in the piecrust).

"Do you like our school?" Edie asks. "You haven't said much about it."

"It's okay." I take a bite of pie. It's really good,

and I wonder if Ms. Whitman bakes a lot. I hope so. "Hey, do you want to come to the beach tomorrow? My surf camp is having an end-of-summer party. Laramie is coming, too."

"Yeah, sure," she says, not taking too long to think about it. I'm glad. I know the beach isn't really her thing. "Who's Laramie?"

"My best friend since fourth grade. And if you like Laramie, you'll like the rest of our friends."

Edie starts to say something but pauses as she looks across the street. Rebekah, the McKees' nanny, pulls her Subaru into the driveway. Before she can get out of the driver's side and open the back door, Stephan bursts from his car seat in back, screaming at the top of his lungs as he hops out. Nicolette sticks her head out of the passenger side, yelling something at him.

"What's up with that kid?" Edie asks, watching Rebekah follow Stephan to the porch. He's pounding his little fists against the front door.

"Stephan McKee. He's a total spoiled brat. His parents aren't very nice. Neither is she," I say as Nicolette steps out of the car.

"No kidding. I hear him screaming constantly." She shudders. "But what's up with her?"

I lower my voice. "Nicolette? She's just never been nice to me. We've been on this street longer than them, but their family always acts like they're the only ones who belong."

Edie frowns. "What do you mean?"

"They just...Nicolette says stuff sometimes. That's prejudiced. Or maybe..."

"Racist?" She says it so plainly, it startles me. Sometimes that seems like a bad word. Like people are more afraid of being associated with it than actually not *being* it.

Across the street, Nicolette glances over at us. There's a second where she pauses, as if maybe she's weighing the idea of making a good first impression on Edie versus being her usual snotty self. She chooses the second option, giving us a long, unsmiling stare before she slams the car door closed and follows her brother and nanny inside.

"Well, she's not friendly," Edie says, making a face. "What kind of stuff has she done?"

"Um, I don't know." I have more stories than I can count on two hands. I've known Nicolette since I was seven years old, which is almost half my life. But now that I have the chance to share all the ways she's been mean to me, I'm feeling shy. There was the thing at the beach, but I don't feel like reliving that right now. Not even for someone who might actually understand. "Lots of little things that just sort of add up, I guess...."

"I believe you," Edie says, looking at me with a serious face. "You know that, right?"

"Yeah, of course." But that's a lie. I'm not used to someone else just knowing what I'm talking about when it comes to things like this. Every time I bring it up with Laramie or one of our other friends, they say it's probably not what I think. That Nicolette or whoever else said something gross or unkind to me probably didn't mean anything by it.

"So," Edie says, "is it true that you were the only black kid in our grade before I got here?"

"Yeah," I say, feeling weird because I haven't told her that yet. So she had to find out from someone besides me. I didn't want to make it into a big deal, but then after a couple of days it seemed weirder and weirder to just bring it up out of the blue.

"My mom told me. I guess one of your dads told her." She chews a forkful of pie and swallows. "I knew there weren't a lot of black people here, but the *only* one?"

"I know." I use my fork to swirl a blueberry through the crumbs on my plate. "There are lots more Asian and Latinx people than black people here, but not a lot. Almost everyone is white."

"Is it weird for you? That I moved here?"

"No! I'm so glad you're here," I say, looking at her until she looks back. I want her to know I mean it. "I don't want to be the only one."

Edie nods and smiles a little bit. "Good."

A YOU-AND-ME THING

THE WATER WILL BE COLD, BUT THE SUN IS HIGH AND
bright for the surf camp party.

I decided to bring my board, so Dad drives Edie
and me over to Laramie's house. Edie stares at the
surfboard with big eyes as Dad and I remove it from
the rack on top of his station wagon and asks if she
can touch it.

"What's it made of?" She runs her fingers lightly
over the front. The board is white with diagonal shades
of blue and green running down the bottom half.

"Epoxy," I say.

Her eyebrows wrinkle. "What's that?"

"I don't really know, actually," I admit. "But all boards used to be made of fiberglass."

"Call us when you're ready to be picked up," Dad says, getting back behind the wheel.

Laramie's front door opens. She steps out and waves at Dad as he backs the wagon onto the street. He toots the horn as he drives away.

"Hey," I say to Laramie. "This is Edie. Edie, this is my best friend, Laramie."

"Cool name," Edie says, and I feel a twinge of something when she says it. I guess I don't expect anyone to think my name is cool, though. It's old-fashioned, like somebody's grandma. Dad's grandma, in fact.

"Thanks," Laramie says. "I like your jeans."

Edie smiles. I did a double take when she walked over to our house this morning. I have on my swim-suit under a long-sleeved T-shirt and board shorts. My wet suit is in the bag slung over my arm. Edie's wearing black combat boots and black jeans with rips in the knees.

"You guys ready to go?" I ask, holding tightly to

my board. I don't know if I'll surf today, but I don't feel right showing up to the party without it.

"It's not even eleven yet," Laramie says. "We don't have to be there right on time, do we?"

"I guess not." But I *like* showing up to things on time. Probably because Elliott and Dad make such a big deal about not being late or keeping people waiting.

"Come inside for a minute? I need to finish getting ready." Laramie waves us through the still-open front door. "Leif is making one of his famous concoctions if you're up for a horror show."

Leif's famous concoctions are weird and pretty gross, like the time he stuffed pizza rolls into a pizza pocket and tried to make a giant calzone out of it all with premade dough and canned pizza sauce.

Today he's making what he calls a Dagwood sandwich. He turns around for a minute to say hey to us and give Edie a nice-to-meet-you smile. Then he goes right back to building what is the tallest, fattest, drippiest sandwich I've ever seen in my life.

"What's in it?" Edie asks, looking enthralled and disgusted at the same time.

"More like what's *not* in it," Laramie says before

she runs upstairs to finish getting ready. Whatever that means. She looks ready to me, with her black-and-red striped swimsuit under a pair of jean shorts.

"Well," Leif says, amused by Edie's amusement, "there's Swiss cheese, American cheese, ham, turkey, tomatoes, corn chips, onions, pickles, mustard, mayo, relish, olives, and roast beef. Oh, and peppers."

All of it separately sounds normal, but looking at it together makes me anything but hungry.

"Are you really going to eat that?" Edie says it exactly like I think girls Leif's age would know to say that to him. Like she thinks he's silly and funny and cute. It's flirty. I haven't figured out how to flirt with boys my own age, let alone ones who are older than me.

"I'm gonna try," Leif says easily. "You want a bite?"

"I'll pass," she says. "I'm still full from breakfast."

I think part of her wants to try it, but probably the part that's worried about getting messy is more important.

"Stop trying to poison the new girl," Laramie says, slipping on her heart-shaped red sunglasses as she comes back into the kitchen.

I look at Edie to see if she's annoyed at being called *new girl*, but she just grins at Leif before tossing her hair over her shoulder.

We leave him with his towering sandwich and walk out Laramie's back door, through the back gate, and over to the stairs that lead down to the beach.

The surf camp is right by the pier, like Irene said. They've set up a volleyball net and two portable grills, and the little kids are building sandcastles and running around one another, screaming and laughing.

As we get closer, Irene waves us over. Her red ponytail swings wildly as she passes sodas from a cooler to kids from the beginner group. We make our way down the beach to her, Edie and Laramie trailing behind me.

"Hey, Alberta," Irene says with a big smile, which she extends to Edie and Laramie. "Glad you all could make it. Jed just fired up the grills, ice cream will be here later, and Leslie is keeping an eye on the surfers. The volleyball net is fair game, too."

Laramie gets a soda, and Edie and I grab waters. I look around, but maybe Laramie was right. Maybe we're too early, because no one my age or older is here. Just the younger kids and their parents. I'm not ready to get in the water yet, so we find a space close to the party but far enough away that we can talk without people hearing us.

Edie spreads out the beach blankets she carried over and we all plop down. Well, Laramie and I do. Edie eases herself down almost...gracefully. She sits with her legs crossed and stares around the beach with her hand over her eyes like a visor.

"So, what do you guys do when you're here?"

"Here?" Laramie looks confused.

"The beach," Edie says, sweeping her arm around. "I mean, when there's not, like, a party going on."

"Oh," Laramie says, and I understand her confusion.

People who haven't ever lived somewhere like here think of the beach as something different or separate from the rest of the town. But the ocean is such a big part of Ewing Beach that I can't imagine a day where I don't think, see, or talk about it. Laramie sees it every single day from her bedroom window.

"Swim, read comics, walk around," Laramie says. "And Alberta surfs, obviously."

"*Obviously*," Edie says in an exaggerated voice.

They look at each other and laugh at the same time. I giggle along with them, but it takes some effort. I guess I don't get the joke.

Edie looks around. "But, seriously, you don't have a boardwalk?"

"Not one like you're talking about. But all the shops and stuff are right up there." I point to Ewing Street behind us.

"Coney Island has *so* much stuff to do," Edie says, digging a tiny hole in the sand with her pinkie. "The boardwalk and the Cyclone and the carousel...And there's the Mermaid Parade every year with bands and costumes and floats."

"How long did you live in New York?" Laramie asks her, and I wonder if she's getting as annoyed as I am that Edie thinks Ewing Beach is so boring.

"My whole life. I've never lived anywhere but Brooklyn. I haven't even lived anywhere except our brownstone...until now."

Laramie nods. "I came here in fourth grade. From Colorado. Why'd you move?"

I give her a look, but she doesn't even glance at me. I told her Edie's parents had split up. I thought she'd know not to ask about it. But Laramie doesn't think much before she speaks. It's never to be mean, but she ends up saying a lot of things she should probably keep to herself.

"My parents are getting divorced." Edie says it like she's unsure. Like she's still getting used to it.

"Sorry," Laramie says. "It's just me, Leif, and my mom. My dad took off a long time ago."

"That sucks." Edie sighs. "My dad is back in Brooklyn. With my brother."

"Is he as annoying as my brother?" Laramie rolls her eyes.

"He's pretty annoying. Especially lately. My mom says it's because he's 'in the thick of being a teenager,' but I'm not going to be a jerk like he is when I'm sixteen."

"Leif is sixteen, too," Laramie says, sitting up a little straighter. "He's not so bad, but he has his jerk moments. And my mom just lets him act that way. She says he'll grow out of it."

"Mine, too!" Edie shakes her head. "But if I say the wrong thing, I'm grounded for a week."

Laramie smiles at her like no one has ever understood her better, and it sends that twinge through me again. How are they already acting like old friends? I look at Laramie to see if she's staring at Edie's black lipstick, but it's like it's something she sees every day.

"Leif is working at the creamery later," Laramie says. "He'll give you a free cone."

"The ice cream there is so good," I say. "Especially the butter pecan."

Laramie laughs. "Alberta should know. It's the only flavor she *ever* gets."

"Because it's the *best* flavor."

But I can't help feeling a little weird that she offered Edie a free cone. And if she were looking at me right now, I wonder if she'd see in my eyes what I really wanted to say: *Leif's free cones are a you-and-me thing.* My gaze slides over to a seagull hopping around a few feet away from us, pecking at the sand for stray bits of food.

"The creamery is way better than Craig's job," Edie says. "He's a barista. I love coffee, but the only thing he ever gave me for free was day-old muffins. If he was in a good mood."

I look over Laramie's shoulder and groan. "What is she doing here?" I mutter.

"Who?" Edie asks, following my gaze.

"Nicolette. Our neighbor."

"Oh. She looks different with sunglasses, I guess."

Laramie turns around, too. And *waves*. I hold my breath, waiting to see what Nicolette will do. Maybe she'll ignore her since she's with her friends, a couple of other soon-to-be eighth graders. But she waves back. And, I'm shocked to see, starts heading our way.

"What are you doing?" I say, pulling my board wax out of my bag.

"Saying hi," Laramie says. "Being nice."

Edie looks back and forth between us. "I thought you didn't like her."

"*I* don't."

"Hey, Laramie," Nicolette says when she and her friends are standing in front of us, blocking our sun. She definitely didn't bring her board. She's not even wearing a suit, just jeans and a tank top. "Hey, new girl," she says to Edie. Finally, she nods at me.

"Hi," I say, forcing myself to form the word.

"I didn't know you'd be here," Laramie says, as if she were hoping Nicolette would be.

"I totally didn't want to come, but my parents made me." Nicolette rolls her eyes. "They said it looks good, or whatever. For me to show up to stuff like this."

Mr. McKee is on the city council, but you'd think he was president of the country with how seriously they all take it.

"We're only staying for a minute," her friend, a blond girl named Shauna, says.

"Yeah, just so Irene sees me here. Then we're going to Gavin's house. His parents are out of town. He's having a barbecue." She looks at Laramie. "You guys could probably come if you want. You too, new girl."

"My name is Edie," she says coolly. "I live next door to you."

"Oh, that's right." Nicolette snaps her fingers like she didn't already know that. "I'm Nicolette McKee."

Laramie looks conflicted. As if she's actually thinking about going to Gavin's party. I definitely can't go. Her house is the only place I'm allowed to be when parents aren't home. Maybe Edie's, too, once my dads get to know Ms. Whitman better.

But I don't *want* to go, either. Laramie is the only reason Nicolette is even talking to us.

I concentrate on waxing my board so I won't watch Laramie's face.

She finally says, "Thanks, but we're just gonna stay here."

Nicolette shrugs. "Suit yourself. Maybe next time."

"Yeah, definitely," Laramie says.

I feel my muscles unclench when Nicolette and her friends move down the beach.

"That was weird," I say to Laramie.

"What? That she invited us somewhere?" Her voice goes up higher than normal. "I think it's nice."

I stare at her, then shake my head. "Never mind." I shouldn't have to remind her of all the times Nicolette has been rude to me. She's *been* there for half of them.

"Hey, Alberta."

I turn around. I've never been so relieved to see Oliver Guzman. He's wearing his wet suit and holding his board.

"Oliver!" My voice is so loud and excited that his eyebrows go up.

"I'm gonna go in," he says. "You want to come?"

I nod, and start tugging on my wet suit. Laramie says hi to Oliver and introduces him to Edie. I tie up my locs and grab my board.

Edie looks from us to Laramie. "Are you going in, too?" she asks her.

"No way. It's too cold to swim most of the time. I'm just here for the sun."

Oliver and I head down to the ocean. The foamy water crashes cold over my feet as the tide rushes in. I usually try to clear my mind before I paddle out, but I'm having trouble today. I don't know why I'm feeling weird that Laramie and Edie are getting along. I should be happy that my best friend likes my new friend. Laramie and I have all the same friends at school. This isn't any different than when Kelsey Romanoff moved here and I met her first and she and Laramie became good friends right away.

It sure does feel different, though.

And then there's the whole Nicolette thing. It's not like Laramie ditched us and went to the party, but it feels like she might have, even if Edie and I didn't want to go.

I look back at them. Edie seemed so interested in surfing before she met Laramie, and now she's not even looking out here. And I wonder if she would've gone to the party with Nicolette if Laramie had decided to.

"Waves are looking good today," Oliver says as we walk into the water.

I nod and breathe in the salty air.

We position ourselves on our boards, lying flat on our stomachs with our legs straight behind us. Finally, I feel comfortable for the first time since I stepped foot on the beach today. The water lapping against my board is calming. It forces me to stop thinking about Edie and Laramie—what they're talking about while I'm gone...and if they're going to start liking each other more than they like me.

I paddle out, watching the waves roll in. Trying to find the perfect one for me.

CONSTANCE

SUNDAY IS MY LAST DAY TO SLEEP IN BEFORE SCHOOL starts, but I wake just as the sun is beginning to rise.

I toss and turn until I hear Dad and Elliott get up. I drag myself out of bed when I hear them mention breakfast.

An hour later, we're headed back home from Rosa's, where we stuffed ourselves with potato-and-egg tacos. Edie is sitting on her front porch with a mug nestled in her hands when we round the corner. Elliott honks the horn.

She stands and waves and keeps standing there

even after we've parked in our driveway. I get out of the back seat and look at her.

"Can you come over?" she calls, cupping her hands around her mouth.

I'm surprised but pleased. After yesterday, I thought she might dump me for Laramie. They were nice when Oliver and I came back after surfing, and Edie asked a lot of questions about it. But I felt strange around them together. It's the same strange way I feel about Laramie now, like she's growing up too fast without me. Like things are changing too quickly and not quickly enough.

"Hey," Edie says when I get to her front porch. "Do you want to come in? I found something in the attic last night, after I got back from the beach. I really want to show you."

And just like that, I feel better. As if the... *thing* that woke me up early and wouldn't let me go back to sleep has vanished. Like maybe Edie doesn't think I'm childish just because I don't wear makeup like her and haven't started my period like Laramie.

"What'd you find?"

She raises her eyebrow and twists her mouth to

the side. Her lips are painted black even this early in the morning. "Come up and see."

Ms. Whitman is kneeling next to the couch in the front room of the B&B, rummaging through a box. Her dark hair is covered in a gray bandana and she's wearing a button-down chambray shirt with the sleeves rolled up. "Good morning, Alberta. How are you doing, honey?" Then, before I can answer, she says, "Please excuse the mess. It's getting better in here, but I still worry we're going to be buried under cardboard for the rest of our lives."

"It looks like you're getting a lot done," I say, because I'm not sure what else to say. It *is* messy and it *does* look like they might be overtaken by boxes sooner rather than later.

She gives me a smile, but also a look that says she knows I'm just being nice.

"Do you want a cup of coffee?" Edie asks.

I stare at her mug. "You're drinking *coffee*?" Elliott gave me a sip of his once and it was awful. Like tar that coated my entire mouth. I had to brush my teeth to get rid of the taste.

"Yeah, I get to drink it one day a week." She laughs at the face I'm making. "Mine is good, though.

I put in tons of sugar and cream. Craig used to get so embarrassed when I ordered at his coffee shop. He's a coffee purist."

"One day a week is fine. You're too young to be getting caffeine headaches like the rest of us," her mother says.

Edie refills her mug and pours me a glass of water before we go up to her room. She grins and pauses as I step on the last creaky stair. "Welcome back to my humble abode."

"Oh my god," I say, looking around. "It's like a completely different room."

"I missed my stuff *so* much." She looks dreamily at the walls, where she's hung framed posters. A couple of them are from musicals, like *Sweeney Todd* and *Little Shop of Horrors*. Another is of a cranky-looking white man with a black mustache and a huge black bird perched on his head.

"Who's that?"

"Alberta! You don't know who Edgar Allan Poe is?"

I shrug. "I've heard of him?"

"We really need to work on your reading list," Edie says, sighing. She points to a silver clothing rack across the room. Almost every single piece of fabric hanging from it is black. "I have all my clothes now. And I got my yearbooks, so I can show you my friends back in New York."

"It looks really...*you* in here," I say, taking in the black duvet on the bed and the black rug with the silver designs. The little hexagonal window across the room is covered with a black lacy curtain.

"Thank you. So, you have to see this." Edie looks at me before crossing the room. She picks up a big metal box with a lock on the front and carries it back to the bed, where we both sit down. "I started looking through some of the boxes that were here when we moved in, and...here."

I look down at the contents, frowning. "Books?"

"Not books—journals. Tons of them. Do you know anyone named Constance?"

I shake my head. That wasn't Mrs. Harris's name, and none of her kids are named that, either.

"Weird. A couple of them have that name in them, but then she stopped signing her name."

"Are you sure they're from the same person?"

"Definitely. They all have the same handwriting."

"Did you read them all?"

Edie pushes the box toward me. "That would

take days. But I did read half of one yesterday. These are *really* old."

I frown. "How old?"

She picks up the book on the very top of the pile and passes it to me.

Even the book looks old. It's bound in a deep blue cloth that's spotted with dark stains. I carefully open it. On the inside cover, in pretty, even cursive, I see:

Constance
1955

I flip to the next page and Edie looks over my shoulder as I read.

January 8, 1955

Oh, I think I adore San Francisco. Mama always said California "wasn't for us," but then who is it for? I believe she doesn't enjoy big cities, but I love it here. The first time I crossed that beautiful bridge, I felt so alive. Sometimes the fog stretches so thick you can hardly see your hand in front of you. People complain, but I don't care if I never see the sun again.

I didn't know if I could do it. But I did. And
it was the best decision I ever made, coming here.
I am home.

Love, Constance

I rest the open book on my knees. "Where did she move from?"

"It doesn't say." Edie reaches for her coffee. "Or at least I didn't get to it yet."

"If she lived in San Francisco, how did all these journals get to Ewing Beach?"

She gives me a look as she slurps from the mug. "It's just a few hours from here. People move all the time. My mom and I moved three thousand miles, and all our stuff got here."

"Yeah, but this was 1955! Our parents weren't even born yet. It wasn't easy to just move around like that...right?"

"I think it just took longer." Edie nods toward the journal. "Read the next ones."

January 12, 1955

I haven't written in a few days because I've
found employment! It's nothing glamorous,

*just enough to pay for my room and meals here
at Mrs. Hansen's. I had enough to get by for a
few more weeks, and I had dreams of exploring
every inch of the city. But Mrs. Hansen seems
suspicious and doesn't like me coming and going
at different times. I don't know why it matters. I
have the money!*

*But I have to respect her rules. I can't afford
to get in any trouble. Not now that I'm all the
way here.*

Love, Constance

January 24, 1955

*I am so tired most evenings that after I eat
supper with Mrs. Hansen and help her clean
the dishes, I'm immediately off to bed. Last
night, I think my eyes were closed before my
head hit the pillow.*

*My work is tiring, but I'm earning a living.
One that Mama would not be proud of, but
it's honest. Mrs. Graham says she wants me to
work for her forever. I laughed when she said
that, but I think she was serious. I like Mr. and
Mrs. Graham perfectly fine, but I hope to move*

on soon. I don't want to clean houses forever,
and I am not interested in serving cookies and
milk every day to little children who see fit to
boss me around.

Every time I want to quit and go back home
and lay my head in Mama's lap, I remember
that I had to do this. This is the right place to be.
Things ~~would be~~ are so much worse back home.

Love, Constance

"How many of these are there?" I ask, looking at Edie.

"So many that I haven't counted."

My questions seem just as endless: *Who was Constance? Why was home so bad that she had to move to San Francisco? Did the little kids boss her around like Stephan McKee?* But for some reason, what I ask Edie is "Why do you think her mom wouldn't want her working for that family?"

"I was wondering that, too." She fingers the edge of another journal with the hand not holding her coffee mug. "Sounds like she was a nanny who had to do a lot of housework. It's not like women could get great jobs back then."

I wonder what Constance *really* wanted to be. I want to know how old she is. And how her journals ended up in this attic, right here in Ewing Beach, after so many years.

"There is one I want to show you.... It's from the same year, but she wrote a *lot* of entries, so I skipped around a bit," she says guiltily, like I'll be mad at her for reading ahead of me. Edie thumbs through a book that looks just like the one I'm holding, only the outside of it is covered in a chestnut-brown cloth instead of blue. She slides her fingers between two pages and passes it over.

I set the new book on top of the one in my lap and begin to read.

September 19, 1955

Today, Mrs. Graham had Mrs. Ogden over for tea. I overheard them talking, and I swear I wasn't <u>trying</u> to eavesdrop, but they weren't <u>trying</u> to be quiet, either. They were speaking about the Negro boy who was killed down South. His mother had an open casket and one of the Negro magazines printed pictures of his "mangled face."

Mrs. Graham said it was a shame, but Mrs. Ogden tsked her. She said maybe if that boy had been minding his own business, he wouldn't have ended up like he did. I couldn't help it—I held my breath as I waited for Mrs. Graham's response.

She told Mrs. Ogden that things are different down there, that we don't really know what it's like when we're all the way across the country. Mrs. Ogden said the Negroes have been getting uppity since they won the Supreme Court case to desegregate the schools. But she didn't use the word <u>Negroes</u>.

I've never heard Mrs. Graham speak so brusquely. "Marilyn, I've told you I don't want that language in my home. Now, if you'll excuse me for a moment."

Then Mrs. Graham came into the kitchen and put another kettle on the stove, though I was standing right there. As soon as I heard her coming, I busied myself with wiping down the counters. But I don't think she even noticed that I was standing right next to her.

Love, Constance

A lump rises in my throat when I'm done reading.

"I think she was talking about Emmett Till," Edie says before I can open my mouth. "Do you know about him?"

"Yeah, my dads are big on black history. They say the schools here don't do a very good job of teaching it."

"My mom and dad say the same thing about New York schools." Edie pauses. "My dad...he's from the South. Something happened to someone in his family, before he was born. Something really bad. Like what happened to Emmett Till, I think. He won't talk about it, and he won't go back there. My grandma still lives in Arkansas, but we never go back to visit. He always flies her up to New York."

"Does your brother know what happened?"

She chews on her lip. "I don't think so. But...I don't know."

I close the book and hand it back to Edie. "I think we should read them all. You're right—San Francisco *isn't* that far...."

Edie raises her eyebrow. I tried to imitate her the other night, when I was getting ready for bed. I stood in front of the bathroom mirror and practiced until

Elliott asked if I was all right in there. But my eyebrow refused to arch in that perfect way, no matter how hard I tried.

"So you think we can find out who this is? Because it's gotta be someone who lived here in Ewing Beach, right?" she says. "At one point? Or maybe they still live here. Maybe Mrs. Harris was keeping them for a friend. Mom said she was pretty old." Edie bites her lip. "I can't believe someone would leave behind something so personal. It feels so . . . sad."

"Are you going to tell Laramie about these?" I ask, looking back down at the journals.

"No." Edie pauses. "Why would I?"

"I don't know. You guys are, like, friends now," I say slowly.

"Well, it's not the same. Whoever this Constance is . . . she wanted to hear what they were saying about Emmett Till. She seems like she cares about these things." Edie looks at me. "I'm not saying Laramie wouldn't care, but it feels different with us, you know? Constance is talking about black people. Black history. And maybe it's not the only journal entry like this. There was a bunch of civil rights stuff going on back then."

I nod, staring down at the box. I can't believe one person could write this much about their life.

"Whoever she is, Constance moved to California from somewhere far away, too," Edie continues. "Her journals being in this attic...I don't know. It feels like a sign."

"Of what?"

"I don't know yet. But I feel like we have to keep reading."

I'm not sure why, but I do, too. I feel like I want to dive into these journals and not stop reading until I've reached the last page of the last book. I want to know why Constance left home, where home was, and how long she worked for Mrs. Graham. I want to know if she ever stood up to anyone who talked bad about black people.

And when I look at Edie, I think she feels the same way.

COUSINS

I USUALLY HAVE FIRST-DAY JITTERS, BUT WHEN I wake up on Monday, I don't feel nervous at all. Just excited. I think maybe it's because I'm starting seventh grade—which isn't as great as eighth grade, but not nearly as bad as sixth. I had a stomachache a whole twenty-four hours before I started school last year. But, really, I think I feel better because Edie is here now.

Normally I'd ride my bike, but Ms. Whitman offered to drive us both since she has to fill out paperwork for Edie, so I ride with them. Dad looked relieved that it's one less thing he has to worry about, since Denise will be here soon and he's still trying to get her room ready.

The B&B is total chaos when I walk over to wait. The front door is cracked, so I peek my head in. The same NPR show my dad listens to every morning is playing loudly in the front room. "Hello?" I call out over the radio voices when I don't see anyone.

A loud series of crashes comes echoing out from the kitchen.

"Alberta, is that you?" Ms. Whitman replies over the noise. It sounds like an entire cabinet of dishes just fell to the floor. "We'll be ready in two minutes! Do you want some water? Orange juice?"

"No, thank you.... Do you need some help?"

"Oh, I'm just fine, honey. Be right there!"

From upstairs, Edie yells down, "Mom, have you seen my black jeans?"

"You just had them on yesterday!" Ms. Whitman yells back.

"No, my *other* jeans!" Edie cries.

Five minutes later, I'm sitting in the back seat of Ms. Whitman's car while she verbally checks off all the things that should be in Edie's bag (tablet, pencils, pens, her new notebook, lunch money). Edie answers with a glazed doughnut stuffed in her mouth. Every time her mother stops at a red light and looks away, she picks up Ms. Whitman's travel mug and takes the tiniest sip of coffee.

Ewing Beach Middle School isn't as big as the elementary, with its sprawling front lawn and play area for recess. And it doesn't have a view of the beach, like the high school. But it's set up on a hill so you have to take dozens of steps or a long semicircle ramp to get to the top. I think it looks majestic, sitting up on the hill like that. Almost like a castle at the top of a mountain. Except it's not mysterious like a big stone castle, since the foyer is an atrium made of glass that lets you see everything. And there's certainly no royalty here.

"You girls go on in and I'll figure out where to park and meet you inside," Ms. Whitman says as she gets to the front of the drop-off line.

Edie chews and swallows the last of her doughnut as we walk up the front path toward the stairs. "She is so not equipped for this."

"What do you mean?" I ask, turning to look back at her mother.

"For trying to raise me and run a business all alone," she says simply.

"I thought she was a stay-at-home mom all your life?"

"She has been, but she and my dad had this whole system worked out with me and Craig in the mornings." Edie sighs. "It's just not the same without him. She even forgot to take a first-day-of-school picture."

"Oh." Now I feel bad that I got annoyed when Dad and Elliott made me pose for mine this morning. I thought I was getting too old for it.

"It's fine," she says, pulling up that same mask she did the last time we talked about her father.

I don't know what to say to that, so we are silent as we make our way up the stairs with the rest of the students. I notice people giving Edie double takes. Whenever people stare at me, I think it's because I look different from most people in town. I hate that feeling—that someone is surprised to see a black person. Like we don't belong in certain areas just because no one was expecting us.

But I forget that Edie is new. A new kid in school is always exciting around here since not many people move to live in Ewing Beach year-round. Maybe they are looking because Edie is black and they weren't expecting to see her. But the looks are curious more than anything else. And Edie doesn't look like anyone else around here, with her dark lipstick, a long-sleeved black dress with a white collar and cuffs, and her black combat boots. (The other black jeans never did turn up this morning.)

Edie acts like she doesn't even notice people staring at her. She breezes through the doors like she owns the place. My stomach flutters and I feel those jitters settling in, right on time. I hope they don't turn into a stomachache. How is the new girl more comfortable than I am when she's only just gotten here?

"Good morning, Alberta," says a voice to my right. "Welcome back."

I look over to see Ms. Franklin, the vice principal. She's standing at the front doors, greeting students as they walk into the atrium. I swear, she's wearing the same outfit she had on the last day of sixth grade: khaki pants with sharp creases down the front, a blindingly white polo shirt, and—wait. Her shoes are new. Every single day last year, Ms. Franklin wore purple Crocs. Even when it was cool out, she wore them with thick wool socks. But these new Crocs are seafoam green, like the pieces of sea glass I used to collect on the beach.

"Good morning, Ms. Franklin." I put my hand on Edie's arm so she'll stop walking. Ewing Beach Middle School isn't the kind of place you can go unnoticed. She'll run into Ms. Franklin nearly every day for the rest of the year. It's best to get this meeting over with.

But before I can say anything, Ms. Franklin's eyes light up. "Oh, this must be our new student."

"Yes," she says. "I'm Edie."

"It's so wonderful to have you here, Edie! Are you two cousins?"

Edie's face twists into a frown that probably matches the one on mine.

"Cousins?" I repeat.

"We just met last week," Edie says. "I moved in across the street from Alberta."

"Oh, yes, of course." Ms. Franklin's face turns a slow and steady pink, like we're watching the sped-up version of someone's sunburn. "I must have gotten my information mixed up. Welcome, Edie! We're happy to have another sea lion in our midst!"

"Sea lion?" Edie mutters when we walk away.

"You didn't look at the website? The Ewing Beach Middle School sea lions." I point to the enormous bronze statue of our mascot, perched on its pedestal in the middle of the atrium. Courtesy of some anonymous alum. I don't really understand donating all that money to make something if you're not going to say who you are.

She snorts. "What's the high school mascot? The manatees?"

"No, the manta rays. And the elementary school is the dolphins."

"Wow. You beach people aren't playing around."

We head to the office where the aides are handing out our schedules for the semester. I get in the line for A–G and Edie stands next to me while she waits for her mother.

"I hope we get some classes together," she says, looking around.

The energy is buzzing more than usual, with everyone reunited after months apart. You can almost tell who's in what grade just by looking. Even the tall sixth graders can't pass for older; they look petrified, like they don't quite know where to stand. I'm so glad to not be one of them this year.

Someone bumps my shoulder and I look over to find Laramie standing in the H–N line next to me. I give her a huge smile, but just as I'm about to open my mouth, I see Nicolette behind her. Of course: Mason and McKee. The lines aren't separated by grade.

I know Laramie had her outfit picked out way before today, but she and Nicolette could almost be twins. They're both wearing jeans with the cuffs rolled up, brightly colored flats, and floral button-down shirts. I look down at my cream-colored dress, ankle boots, and denim vest. I guess I didn't get the memo.

"Back to prison," Nicolette says, rolling her eyes.

Laramie laughs. Edie looks at them curiously. I smile, but only with my lips pressed together and only so Laramie won't say anything. Last time I checked, she *liked* school. She's really good at math, and at the end of sixth grade, she couldn't stop talking about how she was being bumped up to pre-algebra this year, even though that class is for eighth graders.

"I hope I get Mr. Simons for homeroom," Laramie says.

I can't disagree with that. Mr. Simons is the best teacher here, by far. He wears black high-top Chucks, started the rock-climbing club, and has a social media account just for his three-legged cat, Pepper, who lives with him in an apartment above Rosa's Tacos. But I think I like him best because he doesn't treat us like little kids—just people who happen to be younger than him.

Nicolette sighs as their line moves forward. "I'm so jealous he doesn't teach eighth. Simons is a total pushover." She looks at Edie. "You nervous?"

Edie stares back at her, eyebrow arched. "What's there to be nervous about? It's just school."

Nicolette sizes her up for a moment, and I hold my breath. I know that look. It's the one right before she usually says something nasty. She narrows her eyes a bit, but all she says is "I think I like you, new girl."

What? She's hated me the entire time she's known me. She's talked to Edie twice and already likes her? I will never understand Nicolette McKee.

"Edie!" I hear from across the room, then there's a muffled, "Excuse me, I just need to get through— yes, could you just...? Oh, thank you. If I could just squeeze by—"

And then Ms. Whitman is standing beside us, looking even more flustered than she did when she dropped us off. "Hi, girls," she says, smiling at all of us. If she recognizes Nicolette from next door, she doesn't let on. "Ready, Edie? We need to go sit down with the counselor and vice principal for a few minutes. They said you'll get your schedule then."

Edie looks at me as she adjusts the black bag on her shoulder. "Hopefully see you soon," she says before she walks away with her mother.

I'm standing next to my best friend, but as I watch Laramie laugh at something with Nicolette, it sure doesn't feel like it.

By the time we all shuffle down to the lunchroom, I could swear I've been at school for days instead of hours. I did get Mr. Simons for homeroom, and I don't even have to switch classes after that because he's my first-period teacher, too, for English. But I don't have any morning classes with Laramie *or* Edie, which made my heart sink down to my toes when we compared schedules. And I was paired with Mikey Jameson in science lab; Mikey is nice enough, but he constantly smells like onions, even after the big hygiene talks we've gotten in school the last couple of years.

At least there's lunch. I scope out the cafeteria for Laramie and Edie before remembering we're seventh graders now. They're probably outside. Sixth graders and a few of the kids who sit alone usually eat in the cafeteria, but the outside benches are dominated by eighth graders. And somewhere along the way, they decided to let the seventh graders exist in their presence without too much trouble.

The hot-lunch option is always a gamble when it comes to vegetarian food, but today is grilled cheese, so I get in line. I grab a bottle of water and a cup of fresh fruit before I pay, then head outside.

Sure enough, Laramie is seated at one of the far tables, the ones that sit directly in the sun. I pass groups of eighth graders blanketed in shade, and slide into the seat across from Laramie.

"You survived." She's smiling, but I think she's only half kidding about that survival stuff.

"Yeah," I say, but I don't add *just barely*.

It's not that seventh grade is so bad. At least not yet.

We went over the syllabus in each class, and it sounds like we're going to do some interesting things, like studying cells and reading graphic novels. But it seems like there's going to be a lot more homework, and I keep thinking how much more fun the interesting things would be if I had Laramie or Edie there with me.

"Edie and I have homeroom *and* two morning classes together," Laramie says, as if I don't remember from when I saw their schedules earlier. It didn't seem fair, but according to the office, everything is decided by computer. I'm pretty sure they say that just so we won't complain about how unfair it all is.

"I have to sit next to Mikey—" I begin, but I stop when a black leather bag thumps onto the table next to me. I look up. Edie's here. And she looks bored.

"I miss literally everything about my old school." She sighs as she plops down next to me. "No offense. And that lunch line is depressing."

"The food's not so bad here." Laramie nods toward her tray. "The french fries are better than the ones at Shore Burger."

"Everybody's french fries are better than Shore

Burger's," I say, popping one of the cafeteria's into my mouth.

"I guess I'm just missing Brooklyn." Edie smooths down the ends of her long, straight hair. "And people keep saying I look like—"

"Hey, it's Wednesday Addams!" Next to Laramie, Fletcher Thomas straddles the bench, tossing a paper lunch sack on the table. "You guys know each other?"

Edie stares at him.

Fletcher is followed by Jamie Goldstein and Oliver. They plunk their trays down next to us like we do this every day. Laramie looks just as confused as I am. We've known them for years, and Oliver is my friend from surfing, but we've never eaten lunch together. They always acted like they had Very Important Business to take care of that we couldn't be a part of.

It doesn't take long to figure out why they're here. All three of them are staring at Edie like she's one of the characters in the superhero comics they're always passing around.

"Yes, Fletcher," I say, rolling my eyes as I pick up

a triangle of grilled cheese. "Edie's our friend. And my neighbor. Oliver, you didn't tell them?"

He shrugs.

"Edie, see?" she says, making eye contact with each of them. "My name is Edie. After Edith Minturn Sedgwick: It Girl, actress, and muse to the late, great Andy Warhol. Stop calling me Wednesday Addams."

"Who's Wednesday Addams?" Laramie looks around the table at all of us, puzzled.

"The Addams Family."

"Oh, those movies?"

Edie nods. "But it was a TV show first. And before that, it was a comic strip that ran in the *New Yorker.*"

The boys exchange a look. I don't know what they expected from Edie, but it wasn't this.

"Wednesday was the daughter who wore all black and told people exactly how she felt. Real original, guys."

"Fine," Fletcher says, popping open his water bottle. "We'll stop calling you Wednesday."

"To your face," Jamie mutters under his breath.

I guess they're staying, though, because Fletcher crams about half his peanut butter and jelly sandwich into his mouth. He's not even finished chewing when he says, "Are you really from the Bronx?"

Gross. I look down at my fruit cup to get the image of Fletcher's chewed-up food out of my head.

"What? *No!*" Edie's eyebrows knit together. "I'm from Brooklyn."

Fletcher finally finishes chewing and swallows. "Oh man, I totally thought those were the same place." He doesn't even look embarrassed.

"Pro tip: Don't ever say something like that in New York. Some people would fight you for less."

"I'd like to see them try," Fletcher says. Edie stares at his skinny arms.

"Well, California's the best place on Earth," Jamie says.

"Yeah, we've got everything here," Oliver chimes in. "The beach, the mountains, the desert, the best sports teams."

"Please," Edie says. "The Knicks are the greatest team of all time."

"You gotta be kidding me!" Oliver whoops.

The guys grill her about everything, from her

favorite baseball team (the Mets) to whether she likes In-N-Out or Shake Shack better ("Uh, neither," she responds, looking truly offended. "My favorite is the burger at Peter Luger").

Fletcher's lips are twitching. I think he's dying to ask who Peter Luger is, but he stuffs the rest of his sandwich in his mouth instead.

"So, how are you liking it here so far?" Laramie asks, stopping the boys' Q&A session. "I mean, besides the missing Brooklyn part."

"It's okay," Edie says. "Better since I already know you guys. But…"

Fletcher, Jamie, and Oliver take this opportunity to absolutely massacre their lunches. I don't think I've ever seen people eat so fast. Not even them. I guess interrogating the new kid takes a lot of energy.

Edie looks at me. "My English teacher thought I was you."

My eyebrows shoot up. "Mr. Williams thought you were *me*?"

"No way," Laramie says, dragging a fry through her little paper cup of ketchup. "You don't even look alike."

"Well, he called me Alberta." Edie shrugs. "And

when I corrected him, he said he thought I'd done something different with my hair."

"Oh, yeah, that used to happen to me and Alex García," Oliver says, looking up. "I guess two brown kids with *G* names was too much for them to keep straight."

Edie laughs with him, and she doesn't say anything else about it after that, but I can't stop thinking about it for the rest of lunch. Just like I can't stop thinking of earlier, when Ms. Franklin thought we were cousins.

KICKING

I'M STILL FEELING WEIRD WHEN EDIE AND I WALK home from school, but overall, I'd say the day was a success.

Edie is in my math and history classes, and we both chose art as our elective. I have zero classes with Laramie for the first time since she moved here in fourth grade. I know everyone else, of course. It's not like I'm Edie, who had to meet everyone for the first time today.

But I can't believe how cool she was. By the end of the day, everyone wanted to talk to her, and I didn't hear anyone calling her Wednesday Addams in any of our afternoon classes. It was like she's been here her whole life. Like me.

"Everyone's so sporty in Ewing Beach," Edie says as we cross Burton Boulevard. Almost home.

"Not everyone. Laramie's into comics. And zines."

She couldn't stop talking about how she was finally able to take the zine class as an elective. When I saw her after last period, she was so excited about it her cheeks were pink as she talked about brainstorming ideas.

"Yeah, but everyone in my gym class was actually excited that we have to play sports." Edie shudders. As the B&B comes into sight on the corner, she asks, "Want to come over and read more of the journals?"

The journals. I was too excited about seventh grade last night to think much about them, but I do want to read them. I'm about to tell her I need to drop my bag at home and call Dad to let him know where I am when I notice the strange car in our driveway. But it's not actually strange. I know that car.

"Can I take a rain check?" I ask, suddenly wanting to sprint the rest of the way home.

"Yeah, sure." Edie glances at our house. "Whose car is that?"

"Denise and Tim's."

"Who are they?"

My feet feel like they're going to shuffle away without me, but I keep walking next to Edie. Try to play it as cool as she would.

"Family friends." I stop. I don't know how much I want to get into this right now. It's not always easy to explain Denise. Sometimes other people don't make it easy. But I look over at Edie, who hasn't ever judged me or made me feel weird about anything I've told her. "They're, um...Denise is my birth mom...the surrogate for my dads. And she's married to Tim. They live in L.A."

"Oh." Edie's eyes go wide as we stop in front of her house. But not in that annoying way, like some people look when I tell them something about my life. That's always when the string of questions starts. Edie just looks like she's happy that I told her. "How long are they visiting?"

"Denise will be here for a while, but Tim has to go on location for a movie he's working on." I adjust my backpack strap on my shoulder. My toes are positively itching to run across the street. I flex them in my ankle boots. "You can meet her sometime. But I'd better get home to say hi."

"Okay, yeah. See you tomorrow morning?"

"Bright and early," I say before I finally stop fighting it and tear across the street, my backpack thumping against me as I run.

I kick off my boots at the front steps, push the door open, and—

Nobody's here.

"Hello?" I call out. "Dad?"

Nothing.

"Elliott?" I say next, even though I know he's still at school.

Where are they? Did they go somewhere without me? I pad barefoot across the living room and that's when I hear the voices. They're out back.

I hurry to the door and step outside. Dad, Denise, and Tim are sitting under the paper lanterns, glasses of wine and water and a giant cheese board sitting in the center of the table.

Dad looks up at the sound of the door. "There

she is! Were your ears burning? We were just talking about you."

I shake my head, suddenly shy. It was exciting to think about Denise coming, but now that she's here, what if it's weird? I've never lived with a pregnant person before. I've never even lived with a woman.

But as soon as Denise turns and I see her big, warm smile, I feel okay. Happy to see her. She stands and I bound down the porch and across the small yard to hug her. She pulls me tight and all I can smell for a few moments is patchouli and oranges.

"Look at how big you are!" she exclaims, holding me at arm's length. I wonder if she's just saying that. Being back at school confirmed that about 75 percent of the girls in my class are wearing bras now because they *need* to. Not just because they don't want to look like babies. "Oh, I've missed you so much, Alberta."

"I missed you, too," I say, trying not to stare at her belly. Denise is wearing a flowing red caftan with white flowers that looks like it's draped over a beach ball.

"Hey, kiddo," Tim says, wrapping me in a hug of his own. Tim is quiet but kind, and he's so sweet to

Denise in a way I've never seen the boys I know treat any girls. Not even the ones with girlfriends. He's always making sure she's comfortable and that she doesn't need anything, and I can tell by the way he looks at her that he really loves her. It's the same way Dad and Elliott look at each other, sometimes for no reason at all.

We sit down, me taking the empty spot on the bench next to Dad. "I didn't know you were coming today."

"We didn't really know, either," Denise says, glancing apologetically at Dad. "Surprise."

Tim sighs. "The film's production timeline got moved up, so I have to be in Vancouver by tomorrow."

Vancouver. "You're going to Canada?" I know it's just up the coast from here, but it's still another country. That sounds so far away.

"Yeah, right before I'm about to pop out this baby." Denise taps him on the cheek with a long fingernail. "I've been dying to go on one of those trips with him. Vancouver looks gorgeous."

"Hey, we could always have a little Canadian-American baby if you want to take a chance," Tim says with a smile.

"Nope, this baby is going to be California through and through. Just like their mama." Denise rubs the bump under her caftan, then rests her hands on top of it. She looks at me. "How was your first day? I can't believe you're in seventh grade already."

"It was good," I say. "Except I don't have any classes with Laramie."

"What about Edie?" Dad asks, popping an olive into his mouth.

"We have three together." I reach for a piece of manchego and a few green grapes from the cheese board.

"Well, that sounds like a pretty good trade-off." He turns to Denise and Tim. "Edie is the daughter of the woman I was telling you about earlier. She and Alberta became fast friends. We'll have them over for dinner soon so you can meet them, D."

Elliott comes home early and we go out for Thai food. I don't think he and Denise stop talking the whole time. They were best friends on the commune. He met her first, and Denise says the three of them were inseparable once Dad showed up. It's weird to think there was ever a time they didn't all know each other. I've always only had one best friend, but I wonder if Laramie, Edie, and I will ever be that way. *Inseparable*.

When we get back home, I head to my room to do my homework before bed, leaving my dads, Denise, and Tim to sit in the living room, remembering old times. I'd rather be with them, but at least I've heard most of those stories before.

There's a knock on my door just as I'm finishing the reading for science. I say come in, and I see Denise's stomach first, then the rest of her.

"Sorry to interrupt, but I wanted to say good night," she says, resting her hand on her belly.

"Oh, I'm not going to sleep yet." I look at the clock. It's only eight thirty. I still have another hour. Elliott and Dad tacked on another half hour to my bedtime this year. Privileges of seventh grade.

Denise laughs. "No, I meant *I'm* going to bed. This baby and I are exhausted." She lingers in the doorway for a few seconds, and I think maybe she's waiting for me to officially invite her in.

"Do you want to sit down?"

"Sure, if you don't mind. But just for a few minutes, or I might end up falling asleep here." She eases herself onto the end of my bed.

I swing my desk chair around so I'm facing her.

Denise glances at my science textbook. "Homework on the first day? Seventh grade is no joke."

I sigh. "You're telling me."

"But you like it?"

"Yeah, I think so. Maybe."

"Seventh grade isn't easy," she says. "There's something about being your age.... Now, it's been quite a while, but I remember it felt like everything was so different all of a sudden. Like I was going to school with all the same people, but something had changed that I couldn't put my finger on."

I nod, surprised that she just said exactly what I've been feeling for a few weeks now. She hasn't even been here a day. I haven't seen her in months.

She spreads her palm over my duvet. "I hope it's okay that I'm staying with you all for a few weeks. You have a lot going on, with just starting school."

"I'm glad you're here."

Denise smiles as big as she did when I first saw her this afternoon. "Good. I am, too. And I know you have better things to do than hang out with me and my giant belly, but I hope we can spend some time together."

"Me too," I say, shy again. I look at her stomach instead of her face when I ask, "What does it feel like?"

"Being pregnant?" She laughs. "A whole lot of things. I had a tough first trimester. A lot of morning sickness. It's mostly just uncomfortable now. But I like knowing there's something—*someone*—growing in there. And sometimes the baby kicks, which is probably the most amazing thing I've ever felt in my life."

"Did I kick you?"

The question comes out before I even realize what I've asked. My neck turns hot. I wish I could take it back. But when I look at Denise, she's wearing a soft smile.

"Yes, you did. And I thought it was just as amazing. Maybe even more so, because it was the first time I ever felt it."

I've seen pictures of Denise when she was pregnant with me, but sometimes it's still hard to believe I came from her. I feel a ping of warmth in my stomach that she remembers what it was like.

She yawns, her mouth so wide I can see all her molars. "Okay, that's my cue. Time for me to hit the sack." She uses one hand to push off the bed while holding her stomach with her other arm.

"Good night, Denise."

"See you in the morning, sweet girl." She kisses the top of my head before she leaves, closing the door softly behind her.

Tim heads out so early the next day that I'm not up in time to say good-bye.

But I wake up for a few moments before he leaves. I hear gentle scurrying around the house: sleepy toothbrushing, zipping bags, and whispered conversations. My window faces the street, so when Tim is getting ready to drive off, I hear that, too.

"You'll take good care of my girl?" he says, his voice floating through my open window. He sounds more serious than I've ever heard him.

"I'm not a girl, I'm a woman," Denise gently reminds him. "And I can take care of myself just fine."

"Well, we'll be here in case you need any help," Dad says. Even without looking, I can tell he's smiling.

Elliott's voice comes next: "In other words, we got this."

I snuggle back under the covers.

LIVING BEINGS

A COUPLE OF DAYS LATER, ONCE DENISE IS MOSTLY settled in, I go to Edie's house after school.

We're sitting in the attic with a tray of snacks between us. Ms. Whitman is trying out recipes for the B&B, so it's all breakfast foods: honey muffins, eggs Benedict, blueberry scones, and a breakfast lasagna that I can't decide how I feel about.

Two stacks of Constance's journals are lined up next to the tray. I've only read a few entries, but I can already tell her stories are going to be a lot more interesting than most of the books on our reading list this year. I'm not sure our English teacher knows there were books published after 1985.

"So I think we should divide them up and each read them on our own," Edie says, popping a bit of muffin into her mouth. "Then we can reconvene and tell each other what we found."

I take a sip of orange juice from the tall glass on my side of the tray. "But we might miss something if we read separately. Unless...I guess we could take notes."

Edie wrinkles her nose. "I am *not* taking notes, Alberta. Don't we already have enough homework?"

She's not wrong. This was only our third day of school and I'm pretty sure I've already done more homework for seventh grade than in the whole first month of sixth.

"Yeah, but how else will we keep track of what's going on in her life?"

She taps her finger against her temple. "I can keep everything up here. Craig says I probably could've gotten into his fancy gifted school on my memory alone."

"What if we read them separately and *I* write it

all down?" I suggest. "You won't have to do anything except read. Which we already want to do."

"Fine," Edie says after a moment. "But I'm not going in order."

We agree about that. There have to be at least twenty journals here, and the pages are so old that some of the ink is faded and hard to read. Not to mention Constance's loopy writing. We learned cursive in school, but not many people use it except to sign their names. I can barely even read Elliott's signature when he signs my permission slips.

Edie pushes one of the stacks of journals toward me. I figure that's our cue to begin reading, but as soon as I open the one on top, she starts talking.

"Today, someone asked me if I've ever seen somebody get stabbed," she says slowly.

My head whips up. "What? *Here?*"

"No, when I lived in New York."

Oh. I guess that makes more sense, but it's still a ridiculous thing to ask. The thought never even occurred to me when I met Edie. "Who said that?"

"Fletcher." She waves her hand like he and what he said are not important. But she's staring at the set of journals without blinking. "People really don't know anything about New York, huh? It's not some awful place where everyone's terrible all the time. I love New York like it's..."

"Like it's what?"

She shakes her head. "Never mind. It's dumb."

But I won't let it go. "What were you going to say?"

"I love New York like it's family. It's home. I miss it. And I hate when people say stupid things about it. People who've never even been there and only seen it in gangster movies."

"People can be really rude around here," I say. "A lot of them haven't been out of the state... or even the area. They don't know any better."

That's what Dad tells me sometimes when I complain about the things people at school have said to me. It doesn't usually make me feel much better, though. I don't feel any better saying it to Edie, either. And what's the excuse for someone like Nicolette? She and her family go on a huge trip to Europe every summer, and it's like she has a bag full of stupid things that she's just waiting to whip out at any moment.

"I guess," Edie says. But she doesn't look convinced.

My stack of journals is from different months in 1955 and the beginning of 1956. Not necessarily in order, but not too far apart, either. I don't know if Edie separated them that way on purpose, but I like it.

Edie and I ended up talking more than reading, so I stuffed my half of the journals as carefully as I could into my backpack to take home. I was glad I only had to walk across the street. The extra weight was heavy enough on my shoulders to slow me down.

Dad and Denise were just heading out to the market when I got home. They asked if I wanted to go with them, but I chose homework. I want to save the journals to read before bed, and I don't want to have to hurry through my other reading right before.

Now, as I'm finishing the take-home quiz for history, the smell of dinner wafts through the house. I breathe it in, wondering what they're making, when I freeze. Is my nose broken? I smell boiling potatoes, and Dad's favorite herbs—thyme and rosemary—and...meat?

When I get to the kitchen, Denise and Dad are standing over the stove, laughing about something. And cooking a steak.

"What are you doing?" I don't mean to sound so accusatory. But as much as Edie couldn't believe I've never had meat, I can't believe it's being cooked in our house right this minute.

They both turn around. Dad looks guilty.

"It's all my fault," Denise says right away. "I wasn't planning to eat meat while I'm here, out of respect for your home, but the baby wants what it wants."

I think back to the other night, when we went out for Thai food. Tim ordered yellow curry with chicken, but she had a vegetarian dish, same as me and my dads.

"I should've warned you, Alberta," Dad chimes in. Then, looking at Denise: "This is the first time we've ever cooked meat in the house."

Denise lifts the edge of the sizzling steak with tongs and peers on the other side. "Which is exactly why I brought my own pans and utensils."

"You did?"

She looks back at me with a smile. "I'm not trying

to contaminate anything. The smell is strong enough. I know how serious vegetarianism is for you guys."

Still, I don't know how she can eat a steak and not feel bad about it. When I first asked about meat and where it came from and why we didn't eat it, Dad and Elliott showed me a short video for kids that explained everything. We talked about it afterward, and when they asked if I had any questions, my first one was if the part about animals having feelings was true.

"It sure is," Elliott said. "Their feelings and brains might be different from humans, but they still have them. They're living beings, and your dad and I think we should respect that."

I look across the room now, where Dad turns up the fan on the stove hood and slides the patio door wider. I'm not judging Denise for eating meat—most of my friends do. I'm just glad Dad and Elliott aren't going to start, too. That would be another big change around here all within a couple of weeks, and I'm not sure I can handle that right now.

October 31, 1955

I must admit, I was dreading this day for weeks. Mama never liked Halloween. She called it the devil's holiday... but then it never took Mama too long to attribute anything to the devil.

Oh, how I miss her.

Mr. Graham only started his new job at the California School of Fine Arts, but I suppose artists are more understanding, because he was able to leave early to take the children trick-or-treating. I helped them get dressed in the costumes Mrs. Graham spent the past week sewing, and there was only one minor crisis.

Betty didn't want to wear her bunny costume because Mrs. Graham forgot to make a tail. Well, it was too late to get out to Britex and back for the tulle, so I became crafty. I glued together a handful of Mrs. Graham's cotton balls that looked quite convincing, if I do say so myself. Betty and Mrs. Graham were delighted with the fluffy new tail. Crisis averted! Mrs. Graham told me she wasn't sure how they'd ever get along without me.

Patricia asked if I wanted to attend a costume party this evening. When I told Mrs. Graham, she smiled and said I could come in later tomorrow if I wanted. I appreciate the kindness from both her and Patricia, but I declined. I can't get too comfortable. I can't take the risk.

But if I did... if someone figured it out... sometimes I wonder how bad it would be if I were sent back home. I miss my family, and my friends. And Sanford. Sometimes so bad it physically pains me.

Love, Constance

BEACH NIGHT

THE BEST PART ABOUT THE NEW SCHOOL YEAR IS
Beach Night.

It's always held Friday night of the first week, and
the whole middle school is invited. Sixth graders have
to go with their parents, but this year we're allowed to
go unsupervised—as long as we get a permission slip
signed.

I turned mine in the second day of school, but
Edie left hers until the last minute. I waited in the
foyer of the B&B as she tore apart the attic, looking
for the paper. Then she had to bother Ms. Whitman
while she was in the shower. Edie eventually came

downstairs with a water-spotted but signed permission slip.

All anyone can talk about today is Beach Night. Every class buzzes with memories of last year, wondering how it will compare to this one. Especially since most of our parents won't be around.

"Okay, I don't really understand what it is," Edie says when we're sitting at the table we've claimed on the patio outside the cafeteria. She's still avoiding the hot-lunch line like it's poison, but she's made a meal out of yogurt, a small bag of pretzels, and a cup of fresh fruit.

"It's basically a back-to-school carnival, but it's on the beach," Laramie responds. With not having any classes together, all the homework, and getting used to Denise being here, I feel like I've barely seen her all week.

"They set up rides and games," adds Fletcher between gigantic bites of his sandwich. Turkey and Swiss this time.

I jump in quickly. I don't think I can handle seeing him talk with his mouth full for the hundredth time this week. "You can buy carnival tickets to get food at the stands on the beach. And there's a big raffle at the end."

Edie looks suspicious. "What kind of raffle?"

"A bunch of businesses and families donate things," Oliver explains. "Like my dad gives away a free oil change and tune-up at Guzman Auto."

I look across the table at Laramie. "Should Edie and I meet at your house so we can all go together?"

"Actually..." Laramie clears her throat, and I get a sinking feeling that I'm not going to like what she has to say. She must know it, too. She doesn't look at me when she reveals the next part. "Nicolette asked if I wanted to hang out. I think we're going to Gavin's."

Beach Night is only for middle schoolers, but the elementary has their own thing, called Welcome Night. Except theirs is at the school, not the beach, and it's half fun, half parent-teacher meetings. Laramie and I have gone together since she moved here. We went to the beach carnival last year, too, with Dad as our chaperone. I can't believe she made other plans.

"Gavin Reichardt?" Fletcher makes a face.

"What's wrong with Gavin?" Laramie says, not looking at him, either.

"What's *not* wrong with Gavin Reichardt," Jamie mumbles.

"He's kind of a jerk," Oliver says, shrugging like it's common knowledge around Ewing Beach.

It is, though. Mr. Reichardt owns a bunch of buildings around here, and Gavin never lets us forget it. They live in the biggest house in town, so far down the coast from Laramie's that they have their own private part of the beach. Gavin is the kind of person who'll trip a kid and deny it when they fall over his shoe, or shove a random sixth grader into a locker just because he can.

"Well, he's nice to me," Laramie says in a low voice. "He's in my pre-algebra class, and we talk about comics. And Nicolette needs me there for moral support."

I frown. "What kind of moral support?"

Laramie's eyes widen like she's said something she shouldn't have. "Never mind."

Edie dips a pretzel into her yogurt cup. "Does she have a crush on Gavin or something?"

Laramie shakes her head, but I think the red creeping up her neck is the answer to Edie's question.

"Gavin and Nicolette?" Oliver ponders. "I could see it. I mean, both their families think they're better than everyone else."

Jamie snickers.

"They're my friends," Laramie blurts. "You don't have to be rude."

Edie nods at her. "Okay, so we won't talk about them. Tell me more about Beach Night."

But I wish Edie hadn't said that.

I wish we *would* talk more about them. Because I don't understand. Why is my best friend suddenly choosing Nicolette McKee and Gavin Reichardt over me?

Edie brings up Constance on our walk to the beach after dinner.

"Have you been reading the journals?"

"Every night," I say. "What about you?"

She nods, twirling a thick band of hair around her fingers. "They're pretty interesting. It doesn't really feel like homework."

"I know, right? I'm almost at the end of 1955. She seems pretty bored, working for the Grahams."

"The same in the ones I have." Edie nods. "I feel like something bad is going to happen. She keeps talking about having to be so careful."

I got that same feeling, reading through the journals I have. I felt like I couldn't catch my breath and realized I was holding it the whole time I was turning the pages. "I peeked in the ones from 1956, and she's living in Santa Barbara."

"Really?"

"Yeah, and she's only signing her name as *C* instead of Constance. Through the whole thing, I think. I'll try to read more this weekend. We can look her up online, too. Now that we know two places she lived and some of the people she was around... maybe we can find out who she was."

I'll be tired after Beach Night, but I promise myself I'll read a few entries when I get home so we have as much information as possible to work with.

"Definitely," Edie says. "Maybe after dinner tomorrow? Mom says we're having you over."

"You are?"

Edie looks at me funny. "You didn't know?"

I try to think back to the last couple of days. Maybe Dad, Elliott, or Denise mentioned it over breakfast or dinner or before they said good night. But I don't remember anyone bringing it up. Elliott has been so busy with the new school semester and Dad has been distracted since Denise got here, trying to make sure she's settling in okay. He's always fussing over her, asking if she's comfortable or needs anything.

"I guess I forgot," I say as the beach comes into view.

The school sectioned off a whole part of the beach for the carnival booths and games, and the food stands have signs up welcoming Ewing Beach Middle School for the evening. A bunch of sixth graders are here, trying to avoid being seen with their parents as they weave between the booths. We're not the first seventh graders to arrive, and I'm relieved, even though I don't think Edie cares about that kind of stuff the way Laramie and Nicolette would. If Laramie were even here.

"This almost reminds me of Coney Island," Edie says, looking around. "Like, a much smaller version, but still."

I follow her eyes, checking out the booths. There's a bottle toss and football throw, Skee-Ball and whack-a-mole, a giant tic-tac-toe board and hole-in-one, face-painting, and more.

We slowly walk by each one, just looking instead of playing. My game tickets are burning a hole in my pocket, but I don't want to seem too excited. I already feel a little babyish being here when Laramie has someplace better to be.

"What's up, Alberta?"

I turn around to see Rashawn Carlson standing next to me with a redheaded kid named Seth who plays soccer with him.

"Oh, hey, Rashawn."

We're not really friends, but we nod and say hi sometimes in the hallways. Except when he's around the friends who tease him for talking to a seventh grader...and a girl. Then he lifts his chin and walks all slow and cool, like he doesn't see me. I think it should probably bother me more than it does.

Rashawn has coppery skin, and he's wearing a blue Dodgers cap tonight over his close-cropped reddish-brown hair. He looks at Edie before his hazel eyes drift back to me.

"What are y'all up to?"

"Um, just walking around, I guess."

"Cool." He looks at Edie again. "Hey, you're new, huh?"

I give him a look. He knows she's new, just like everyone else at Ewing Beach Middle School knows. It's hard to miss a new kid in a town this small, and it's especially hard to miss a new kid who also happens to be black.

She nods. "Yeah, I'm Edie."

"I'm Rashawn. This is my boy Seth."

"Hey," Edie says to him.

Seth kicks his chin up, then sets his eyes on the booths behind us. He's not much of a conversationalist.

"You like it here so far?" Rashawn asks her. "In Ewing Beach, I mean."

Edie shrugs. "It's all right."

"Yeah," he says. "It's all right."

Then it's quiet for a long time and it's *so* awkward until Seth finally says, "I'm starving, man. Want to hit up Shore Burger?"

"Uh, yeah," Rashawn says, even though I don't think he wants to go to Shore Burger at all. I'm pretty sure he'd rather keep standing here with his hands shoved in his pockets, staring at Edie. He glances away every few seconds, but he can't stop looking at her. "You want to go get some burgers with us?"

"I'm not really hungry," Edie says. She looks at me. "Are you?"

"Not really. I just ate dinner."

"Okay, well. Cool," Rashawn says again. He clears his throat. "Maybe we'll see y'all around."

He and Seth tromp away in the sand.

"He has *never* come up to talk to me like that," I say, watching them.

Edie twists her mouth to the side. "Maybe it's different now that you're in seventh grade?"

"I don't think so." I shake my head. "I'm pretty sure it's because he thinks you're cute."

"But he barely said anything."

Just then, Rashawn turns around, his eyes on Edie again. She notices and looks down, hiding behind her curtain of hair. But I can see the way her lips turn up at the corners. And before he turns around, she looks back at him without hiding her smile.

After Rashawn and Seth leave, Oliver and Jamie show up almost immediately to take their places.

"Where's Fletcher?" I ask, my eyes darting around the carnival. I get the feeling he's somewhere near the food.

"His grandparents are visiting. His parents wouldn't let him skip dinner," Oliver says. He tilts his head toward the direction Rashawn and Seth just walked. "You been hanging out with them?"

Edie looks down the beach, squinting, as if she's forgotten who we were just talking to. "Oh. They came up to introduce themselves."

"Eighth graders, man," Jamie mumbles.

I stare at him. "What about them?"

He rolls his eyes. "You guys are obsessed with hanging out with them."

"I think you have us confused with Laramie." I frown. "And what do you care? You wouldn't even eat lunch with us until this year."

Jamie looks like he wants to protest, then realizes I'm right and keeps his mouth shut instead.

Oliver shrugs. "We got bored."

"Gee, thanks."

"I didn't mean it like that," he says, his tan skin deepening a shade. "I think...I mean, you're really the only girls worth talking to in seventh grade. Who will we have if you start hanging with the eighth graders?"

"Sixth-grade girls?" Edie says with a straight face.

The boys look like they've been slapped. Edie and I catch each other's eye and burst out laughing.

"Come on," she says. "I want to try some of these games."

The four of us use all our tickets over the next hour, playing every single one. I have so much fun with them that I almost forget about Laramie not being here. Oliver and Jamie pretend to be too cool to get their faces painted, but Edie chooses a single black heart while I pick a golden sun with sweeping rays. Edie shows me the best technique to play Skee-Ball, and Oliver challenges all of us to a whack-a-mole tournament, which Edie calls "totally savage but hilarious."

We spend the last of our tickets at the bottle toss, trying to get the rings to land around the necks of the glass bottles. Edie concentrates so hard, the tip of her tongue sticks out of the corner of her mouth, but she loses on her last turn.

"Oh well," she says, glancing at the wall of prizes before we walk away to let the boys have their turn.

"What did you want to win?" The prizes don't look like anything she'd want—things like stuffed animals, glow bracelets, glitter pencils, and erasers that smell like fruit.

Edie shrugs. "Nothing. My dad couldn't leave Coney Island without playing the ring toss. He almost never got a ring around the bottle, but he'd always let me play his last two turns. And I'd almost always win and he'd tell me I saved the day. He was obviously throwing the game just to make me feel good, but he liked it, so I pretended not to notice."

"How is your dad?"

"Fine, I guess. He's been so busy with this new album that we can only talk for a few minutes at a time. Craig said he's practically living in the studio." She blinks at me. "What?"

"What what?"

"You're looking at me strange. Like you feel sorry for me."

"I am not."

"You *are*, Alberta." She shakes her head. "Don't do that, okay? I'm fine. Everything is fine."

"I know." Even though the way she says it makes me think it's not true at all.

Jamie and Oliver finish their games empty-handed. "These things are totally rigged," Jamie says, scowling.

We walk around the carnival one last time, but we've used all our tickets and things are starting to wind down. I keep scanning the crowd. Maybe Laramie will change her mind and show up after all. But I never see her.

November 15, 1955

Yesterday, I did something foolish.

I didn't mean to, but does anyone ever set out to be foolish? Well...I think I know what Papa's answer would be.

I don't often stop at a newsstand, but yesterday, my feet took root right in front of the one I pass each day on my way home. I scanned the rows. There was the <u>San Francisco Chronicle</u> and the <u>Oakland Tribune</u>, the papers in languages I don't speak...and the <u>Sun-Reporter</u>. I glanced around to see if anyone noticed me, but everyone simply hurried by, eager to return home.

Right there on the front page was a story about how slowly desegregation continues to progress in the South. But this wasn't the usual article blaming Negroes for all their troubles. This was written <u>by</u> Negroes, <u>for</u> Negroes, and it was published here in San Francisco. Detailing everything that was happening down in Dixie.

"You okay, missy?" the man in charge of the newsstand asked me.

I said I was fine and then I quickly folded the paper in half and brought it to him. "I'd like to buy this, please."

He unfolded the paper and looked at the front. He stared at me. I wanted to look away, to run away. But I knew I had to look right into his eyes.

"What's a pretty girl like you doing with this? You know it's a Negro newspaper, missy?"

My fingers trembled. I clasped them behind my back. "It's for our housekeeper."

"You runnin' around buying things for your house gal?"

"It's part of her wages," I said, standing tall. Proud. "We like our help to be educated."

"Don't see why they need their own paper when all their problems always stinkin' up ours." He shook his head and grunted. "That'll be ten cents."

I dropped a dime in his hand, took my paper, and walked away with my head held high. But my heart was pounding like a drum, and as soon as I turned the corner, I stuffed the paper under my coat.

I read it after my bath, by the lamp in my room. Page after page of sympathetic stories about the Negroes and their plight. How hard things have been for them. How they have so much further to go to achieve equality.

I wept as I read every single word.

Before I went to sleep, I slid the paper under my mattress so Mrs. Hansen wouldn't find it.

Love, Constance

LOOK-ALIKES

THE FOYER AND FRONT ROOM OF THE B&B ARE totally transformed when Dad, Elliott, Denise, and I show up for dinner the next evening.

All the clutter and boxes have disappeared. I finally see the floral print of Mrs. Harris's couch and chairs. Elliott looks approvingly at the oversize art books spread out on the coffee table, and Dad compliments the framed prints hung on the walls.

"It's a start," Ms. Whitman says. "I think this is a bigger undertaking than I realized."

"I know the feeling," Denise says, rubbing her

belly. "Hi, I'm Denise Kaplan. I've heard so many wonderful things about you."

Edie's mother grins. "Calliope Whitman. And likewise, Denise. Welcome to my work in progress."

"I think it's lovely." Denise smiles back at her. "I've always dreamed of living in a house like this."

Over dinner, Ms. Whitman asks Denise what she does.

"Oh, *thank you*," Denise says after she's finished chewing a bite of eggplant parmesan.

Ms. Whitman gives her a puzzled look.

"Since I've been pregnant, no one ever asks about *me* anymore." She looks at Elliott and Dad with narrowed eyes. "Even you two constantly talk about the baby."

"We're excited," Elliott says with a shrug. "And besides, we know everything about your life."

Denise makes a face at him before she turns back to Ms. Whitman. "I'm a freelance journalist. I used to work as a reporter for the *San Francisco Chronicle* when Tim and I lived up north. I mostly covered crime and local politics."

"I'm sure that was never boring."

"Never," Denise says, laughing. "I miss it sometimes. Now I mostly write magazine features. Some profiles."

"What do you miss about it?" Edie asks. Sometimes I don't think she's paying attention, but she's always listening. Quietly watching.

"About what I used to do?" Denise sips her peppermint tea. "The research. Feeling like I've reached a roadblock with a story and then realizing there's another avenue I haven't explored...another way to get to the truth."

"It's essential work," Ms. Whitman says. "I've tried to convince my son to go into journalism, but he's only got eyes for neuroscience."

"There's certainly more money in neuroscience. But I love what I do. That's the most important part."

After dinner, Edie and I go up to the attic. I didn't want to lug the journals with me, so I made notes of the details that might help us figure out who Constance was.

"I found something in one of the books," Edie says before I've even sat down. "I wanted to show you all day, but I figured it was best to wait until now."

She slides something out of a black clothbound journal and hands it to me. A black-and-white photograph. The woman in it is pictured from the shoulders up, and like the pages in the diaries, the photo is faded and fragile. She's wearing a soft-looking sweater and a bow in her dark hair, which is short and curled above her shoulders. I wonder what colors the sweater and bow are. She is white and her smile is big, with a slightly crooked front tooth, and her eyes look light-ish. Probably not blue, but maybe hazel or green.

"Who is this?" I ask, then turn it over and gasp. "It's *her*?"

"I guess so," Edie says. "Does she look like you thought she would?"

"Not really?" I don't know what I expected her to look like. Maybe not like this, even though I'm not sure why. But it's right there on the back of the picture: *Constance, 1954*. The year before the first journal. When she was still living with her family.

"I wonder if she still looked like this after she moved to California," Edie ponders, staring at the photo.

"What do you mean?"

"Well, it seems sort of like she reinvented herself. With whatever secret she's hiding. Maybe this is just a reminder of what she used to look like."

"Maybe." But what could she have done to change what she looked like? Dyed her hair? And what was she hiding?

"She looks nice," Edie says. "It doesn't surprise me that she cares about other people so much."

Edie's right. She does look kind. Her eyes, especially. Still, I can't believe she's the woman whose life we've been reading about. For some reason, I guess I thought she could've been black, with the way she talks about black people and knows our history. I don't think I'll be able to get her face out of my mind whenever I open a journal.

"I did some research on Santa Barbara." Edie picks up her tablet. "Did you know that my namesake was born there?"

"Who?"

"Edie Sedgwick! And the Chumash tribe lived in the area for *thirteen thousand* years before white people got here."

"It's really pretty in Santa Barbara," I say. "Dad and Elliott have friends there."

Edie slides her tablet toward me. "Do you want to look things up? I don't like typing. And you already have notes."

I unfold the piece of paper I brought with me and set it on my lap. The background of the tablet screen distracts me. It's pitch black with a big, white moon in the center. Simple, beautiful, and slightly creepy.

"Is it weird having Denise stay with you?" Edie asks.

I shrug. "No, not really. She's easy to get used to."

"Even eating dinner with her and your dads? It's not weird having an extra person there?"

"No, it's kind of better, actually," I say slowly. "They don't ask me as many questions about school."

"I don't know if I'll ever get used to not eating dinner with my dad." Edie's voice is quiet. "It's not like he was even there to eat with us all the time, but he'd warm up a plate when he got home later. Or if he was out of town, he'd call right before we were about to eat so it almost felt like he was there at the table. I just...I knew when I'd see him again. And it's different now."

"Have you talked to him lately?" I don't know if I should be asking, but if I were missing someone, I think I'd want to talk about them.

"Yeah, we talk almost every day. I mean, we text, mostly. He's busy, and the time difference is hard. But he's going to come out here as soon as he can. I might go spend the weekend with him in L.A. sometime."

"That would be fun."

"Yeah, it will be." She pauses, combing her fingers through the ends of her hair. Then she says, "You look like her."

I glance at Edie. "What?"

"Denise. You look like her."

"Oh."

"Sorry. Am I not supposed to say that? I know she's not really your mother...."

I shrug. "She's not *not* my mother."

"Well, you look alike." Edie smiles. "She's pretty. And really nice."

I nod. Then I focus on the tablet again. I don't know what to say. I know I look like Denise. Dad and Elliott mention it sometimes, how I'm looking more and more like her every day. It's a *good* thing, but it's also weird. Even though she's my biological mother, that's all we share. We've never lived in the same house...well, until now. But she didn't raise me. So it's strange knowing there's someone out there with my face when I don't call her Mom.

"Let's start on this," I say, looking down at my piece of paper. I've only written a few things on it, anything that could help us figure out who she is:

1. Constance
2. San Francisco
3. Mr. and Mrs. Graham
4. Mrs. Ogden
5. Betty Graham
6. California School of Fine Arts
7. Santa Barbara
8. State Street
9. Schiff's Department Store
10. Sanford

I hold the paper out for Edie to see.

"That's a lot of *s* words," she observes.

I spend the next few minutes typing in all the words: together, separately, in different order. Every search brings up a ton of results, but nothing that really means anything.

Edie sighs, frustrated. "Seriously, *none* of these things are helping? How is that possible?"

I look up each term separately again, but I don't find anything new that I missed. None of the Constances that come up are our Constance. They're either way too old or too young. And besides, we don't even know her last name. Or Sanford's, whoever he is.

"We need more information," I say.

"How are we going to figure it out if we can't do it this way?" Edie frowns. "Everything is on the internet."

Suddenly, Denise's words flash through my mind.

Feeling like I've reached a roadblock with a story and then realizing there's another avenue I haven't explored... another way to get to the truth.

I tap the pen against the paper. "Maybe there's another way."

December 5, 1955

*I've begun purchasing the Negro newspaper
every week now. I visit the same newsstand so I
won't cause additional suspicion. The man still
grunts at me each time, yet he doesn't further
complain.*

*But today, he spoke to me. "They reportin'
about that old gal who wouldn't move on the
bus?" He pointed to the <u>Sun-Reporter</u>.*

"Excuse me?" I said.

*He slid a copy of the <u>New York Times</u>
my way, open to an article with the following
headline: BUSES BOYCOTTED OVER RACE
ISSUE; MONTGOMERY, ALA., NEGROES PROTEST
WOMAN'S ARREST FOR DEFYING SEGREGATION.*

*My breath hitched in my throat and I felt the
man staring. I quickly pulled a fresh copy off the
rack and placed it on top of the <u>Sun-Reporter</u>.
"I'll take one of these, as well."*

*He shook his head. "Better be careful with
that help of yours. Those people gettin' too uppity.
Demandin' so much, like the world owes 'em."*

I handed him a quarter, tucked the papers
under my arm, and began to walk away.

"Wait a second, missy. I still owe ya—"

"Keep the change," I called over my shoulder.

I won't miss the five cents. I couldn't stand to
be near him another moment.

Before bed, I read the article. It detailed
the arrest of Mrs. Rosa Parks, a Negro woman
who refused to sit in the back of the bus, where
Negro passengers must ride in Alabama. The
article says the Supreme Court is already set to
hear a case about bus segregation, from South
Carolina. I've copied down part of the article
because I still can't believe it's true.

Other Negroes by the thousands,
meanwhile, found other means of
transportation or stayed home today
in an organized boycott of City Lines
Buses, operated by a subsidiary of
National City Lines at Chicago.

The manager, J. H. Bagley,
estimated that "80 or maybe 90
percent" of the Negroes who normally
used the buses had joined the boycott.
He said "several thousand" Negroes
rode the buses on a normal day.

Mama always used to say, "Real change
take too long to come. Ain't never gonna see it in
my lifetime, and probably not in yours, girl."
But maybe Mama was wrong. Because
this ... this is something. I bet Sanford would be
part of the boycott if he lived in Montgomery. I
am sure he is so very proud of it.

                                    Love, Constance

13

POSER

DAD'S ART GALLERY IS POPULAR WITH LOCALS AND tourists, but he only hosts a couple of exhibit openings a year. So when he does, we get all dolled up and make a night of it.

Usually it's just Dad, Elliott, and me, but this time it's a whole crew: the three of us, plus Denise and Laramie. I haven't really had a chance to talk to her since Beach Night, which was only a few days ago, but seems like forever. There's always someone around at lunch or in the hallways, and we've been so busy with homework that we barely have time to text. I miss her.

"How was Gavin's?" I ask when we're in my room, getting ready. I can't decide if I should wear a dress or a skirt.

Laramie is wearing a short denim skirt and a baggy white sweater that falls off her left shoulder. I keep looking at the deep purple of the tank top strap peeking out, but really, I can't get over her skirt. I've never seen her wear one so short, and her legs look miles long.

She shrugs, picking at her fingernails. "It was fine, like I told you."

"Yeah, but you didn't say how it *really* was." It's not every day that we hang out with eighth graders. Well, I guess I *never* have.

Laramie is quiet, like she's thinking about the best way to say it. "It was sort of fun, but..."

"But what?" I ask, holding up an oatmeal-colored sweater. I toss it on the floor. It looks too much like Laramie's.

"Once we got there, Nicolette just sort of ignored me."

I look at her in the full-length mirror on the back of my closet door. "So why'd you stay? You could have come to Beach Night."

"I don't know. It just felt like once I was there, I shouldn't leave. They were nice enough to invite me."

"And then ignore you all night," I mumble.

"You don't know what it's like, Alberta." Her voice is irritated, like she's been sounding more and more lately.

"I don't know what *what's* like?"

She shakes her head. "Forget it."

I don't want to forget it, though. I want to know exactly what she means, because she's my best friend. Because we're supposed to tell each other everything. Even the uncomfortable things.

But just then, Elliott raps on my bedroom door and says, "Time to head to the gallery, ladies."

I still haven't decided what to wear. Laramie practically runs to the door, as if she's grateful for the escape.

Dad's gallery is located on Ewing Street, but it's positioned at the end of the main drag. A few buildings down from Coleman Creamery and Rosa's, but not as far as the post office and library.

A big chalkboard sign out front advertises in perfect, swirly script the opening show for the artist:

Verbena Fujimoto. Inside, the single room glows with lighting that accents the paintings perfectly hung on the walls. Dad's employees, Judith and Wyatt, are dressed in all black, setting up the table of drinks and hors d'oeuvres.

Elliott heads straight for the food.

Dad sighs. "Honey, that's for the guests. We have dinner reservations in two hours."

"No one's going to miss a handful of cheese and crackers," Elliott says, already filling a tiny napkin. "I had to come straight from school—I can't wait two hours."

Dad produces a protein bar. "And I came prepared."

Elliott grumbles and takes it, but only after he inhales three cubes of gouda first.

"Where's the artist?" Laramie asks, gazing around at her paintings.

As if she heard Laramie talking, a tall woman with a shaved head enters from the back room. She's wearing a floor-length sequined dress the color of pine needles and fringed leather earrings that hang to her shoulders. She has creamy white skin and lips painted candy-apple red.

"Wow," Denise breathes on the other side of me. "I can't believe she's really here."

"You know her?" I ask.

"She started out as a graffiti artist, and then people started paying attention. Now she's doing gallery shows," Denise says in a low voice. "Technically still up and coming, but all the true artists know Verbena Fujimoto. She's going to be huge in, like, six months."

Laramie and I walk around the gallery, checking out the paintings before the opening starts.

"I still don't really know if I *get* art," she says, tilting her head to look at a piece. It's the outline of a girl filled with all kinds of objects against a hot-pink background.

"Elliott says it's about analyzing the circumstances around the art."

Laramie squints at me.

"Like...when it was made, who made it, and what their influences were." I guess I remember more than I thought from when he and Dad get into their big discussions. Sometimes they last for hours.

"Oh." She regards the piece again. "Well, what if you don't know anything about it and just like the way it looks?"

"That's what Dad says art is all about. How it makes you feel. And it's what Ms. Rabinowitz said the first day of school."

"It's like at Gavin's house, there's all this expensive art we couldn't touch, but it was honestly pretty boring. Nothing like this. I thought Gavin was going to kill Davis for bumping into a table with a sculpture of some old dude." She snorts at the memory. And it's weird that Laramie is laughing about something I wasn't there for.

"Is he actually nice to you?"

"Who, Gavin?" She stares at the painting a few more seconds before she looks at me. "Yeah, he is. He's actually the only one there who seems to care about who I am. He asks questions and stuff."

I nod. That's not the Gavin I know, but at least he's being nice to Laramie. Even if I don't understand why she's hanging out with them, I don't like the idea of them being rude to her.

"They were talking about Edie," she says.

My eyebrows knit together. "About what?"

Laramie shrugs. "Just like they talk about any new kids."

But I know Nicolette and Gavin, and that doesn't mean anything good. "What did they say, Laramie?"

"Just...Nicolette called her a poser."

I wrinkle my nose. "What's that supposed to mean?"

"Like, the whole goth-girl-from-New-York thing. It's kind of a lot."

"But that's who she is. You should see her room. I don't think she owns any color that isn't black, white, or silver."

"Is that *really* who she is? I mean, I don't know a lot of black people who dress like that."

I freeze. "So?"

"It's just...what if she reinvented herself to come out here?"

Reinvent. That's the word Edie used when she was talking about Constance. And I don't think Laramie is right, but I can't help remembering how Edie immediately wondered if Constance had changed her whole look when she moved out here. That's not what Edie did, too...is it?

"She didn't," I say, shaking the thought from my head. "I've seen pictures of her with her friends back in New York."

"Okay. Well, it's still a little strange. The way she looks."

"And honestly, Laramie, how many black people do you even know?"

She frowns at me. "What's that supposed to mean?"

"Just, like…you don't know how every single black person dresses. Maybe it's normal in New York City."

Laramie presses her lips together and wrinkles her nose like she's smelled something sour. That expression reminds me of Nicolette so much that I cringe, but then, when I keep watching her, I see something else cross her face. She looks…uncomfortable.

"I thought you liked Edie," I say, thinking back to that day on the beach when I was the one who felt left out.

Laramie brings both of her shoulders up in a shrug. "She's fine, but I still think her black lipstick is weird."

"You're being kind of mean." I wish my voice didn't wobble. But I hate this. The way she's talking reminds me of Nicolette, too. Laramie used to like Edie, and she didn't say any of this when she first met her. Was she really thinking this the whole time, or did Nicolette change her mind?

"Oh, come on. You just met her." Laramie laughs like we've been joking around this whole time. It makes my stomach hurt. "What, is she your best friend now?"

She says it like it's a joke, but there's something on the edge of her voice. Something that makes me think she's not kidding at all.

"She's my *friend*. She's not a poser. You don't even know her."

And I really hope you're not turning into Nicolette McKee.

After the opening, we go to dinner with Verbena Fujimoto. Elliott orders half the menu while Denise asks Verbena question after question about her art and life. Dad monitors his phone for social media about the event, interrupting their conversation every few minutes to show them a new picture or post.

Laramie and I barely talk. I see Dad looking over at us a few times, but I don't meet his eye. We never used to have moments like this, but it's happening more and more lately. I don't like the tension. It's so thick I can practically see it hanging above us, and no matter what, I can't win. I don't want Laramie talking about Edie, but I don't want her to think I like Edie more than her.

In the car, I notice Denise peeking back at us a couple of times. I sit silently between Laramie and Elliott.

"Thanks for letting me come tonight, Mr. Freeman-Price," Laramie says when we drop her off after dinner. "It was fun."

But I think everyone in the car can tell she doesn't mean that last part.

"Hey, are you coming to the surf festival on Saturday?" I ask before she closes the door.

"I don't think so," Laramie says after a moment. She looks at her shoes. "It's Nicolette's birthday, so..."

So she's going to her party without me. I wonder if it's at Nicolette's house. Her parents used to make her invite me, but I guess the rules changed last year. I watched from my bedroom window while Rebekah tied balloons to the mailbox and draped a metallic banner over the front door. Then I watched as a bunch of people from school showed up with wrapped presents and gift bags.

"Oh, okay." I swallow. "Well, is Leif still going to the festival?"

"Yeah, he's competing."

Laramie still isn't looking at me, probably because she's breaking another one of our traditions. We always used to go to Pismo Beach to watch Leif compete in the preliminary round on Saturday. He usually made it to the finals on Sunday, too, and a couple of years ago, he took home the top prize in his age group. This year, Irene put together a group of kids from surf camp who want to go. Laramie never said she was coming, but when I told her, she said it sounded fun. I guess I thought that meant she would come with Leif and their mom since we've always done everything together. Elliott says you should never assume anything, but it's hard not to when it's your best friend since fourth grade.

A thick silence hovers between us, and I don't like it. But I don't know how to fix it.

Laramie finally looks at me before she heads up the path to her house. "See you at school tomorrow."

Dad waits until she's inside before he drives away. Elliott squeezes my arm. "Have a good time tonight, Al?"

"Mm-hmm." Then, repeating Laramie, I say, "It was fun."

I keep forgetting to do things before I go to bed.

First, I brush my teeth, but I forget to swish with the fluoride rinse that sits on the counter. Then, as I'm getting ready to curl up in bed with Constance's journal, I remember my sleep cap is in the bathroom, where I left it this morning.

As I make my way past Denise's cracked door for the fourth time in ten minutes, she calls my name. I poke my head in.

"Everything okay?" she asks from the bed, where she's rubbing lotion into her elbows.

I nod, but it must be clear to Denise that everything is not okay. She gestures for me to close the door and pats the empty space next to her on the bed.

I tentatively perch beside her. I try not to look around too much so she won't think I'm nosy, but I haven't really been in here since she moved in. Instead of the office/guest room, it looks more like a real bedroom. The desk is still here, but Dad moved the computer. Stacks of books line the nightstand

and desktop, and Denise has set up incense and oils on top of the dresser. From the open closet door, I see a row of colorful caftans and flowing tops.

"Did you really have fun tonight?" she asks, scooping her fingers into the lotion jar.

I shrug. "Kind of. I liked meeting Verbena Fujimoto. She's probably the coolest person who's ever been to Ewing Beach."

"Isn't she?" Denise says wistfully. "It was such a joy to meet her. You know, they always say not to meet your heroes, but she was everything I thought she'd be. Maybe even better."

The only heroes I have are surfers, and most people haven't heard of them like they know singers or actors. My favorites right now are Coco Ho and Sage Erickson. Some of them, like Wendy Botha, aren't even surfing anymore, so I only know them from old videos Irene tells us to find online.

"Things with Laramie all right?" Denise presses.

"Yes. No. I don't know." When Denise doesn't say anything, I go on. "Everything used to be fine between us, but now it seems so different."

"Different how?"

"Well, she hangs out with Nicolette McKee sometimes."

"McKee?" Denise frowns, trying to place the name.

"The family across the street."

"Oh, that's right." Her frown deepens. "They've never been very neighborly, if I'm recalling correctly."

"That's them. Nicolette is in eighth grade, but she and her friends like having Laramie around, so Laramie has started hanging out with them."

"And she's leaving you behind?"

I nod. "Sometimes I wonder if it's because she's . . . growing so much faster than I am."

"Growing?"

"She already got her period. And she's so tall now. I feel like such a baby next to her sometimes."

"Oh, Alberta. I know it's hard, but try not to focus on that too much, okay?" She pauses. "I got my period much earlier than everyone else in my class— when I was ten. All I wanted was to be like the other girls. I felt so different."

"Really?"

"Really. And, you know, sometimes growth comes

faster on the inside. Your body is doing exactly what it's supposed to do."

My skin is hot, even though Denise knew just the right thing to say.

"What about Edie?" Denise asks. "You two seem to get along well."

"We do. But tonight... Laramie told me Nicolette and her friends were talking about Edie."

"What did they say?" Denise asks, twisting the top onto the lotion jar.

"That she was a poser. They think her whole look is fake."

I'm pretty sure the look on Denise's face is the exact one I gave Laramie at the gallery. "Why would they think that?"

"Because they don't know any black people who dress like her or who like the same things as her."

Denise scoffs. "You have to be kidding me. *That* was her reason?"

I nod again, pulling at a loose thread on the seam of my pajama pants. Denise is quiet for a moment. For so long that I wonder if maybe I shouldn't have said anything. She has enough on her mind, I think, as her protruding belly catches the corner of my eye.

But then I feel her hand, gentle under my chin. When I look up to meet her gaze, she's giving me this expression that's somewhere between sadness and a smile.

"I don't know all the facts or everyone involved," she says softly. "But I do know that what they said about Edie is not okay. People who say things like that usually haven't been exposed to other races or cultures. And, unfortunately, they think it's fine to pass judgment on a group of people they know nothing about."

"Yeah, I kind of told Laramie the same thing."

Still, Denise's words send a flood of relief swimming through me. What Laramie said has been bothering me for hours, but I thought maybe I was taking it too seriously. She says I do that sometimes. And usually, when it has to do with race stuff, the only black people I have to ask are Dad and Elliott. They help me talk things out when they can, but they don't always get why something is important to me. Sometimes they tell me I should just stop worrying about things, even though it's not always that easy.

"Also," Denise continues, "a big part of me can't help wondering if Laramie told you that because she's a bit jealous of your friendship with Edie."

I shake my head. "We're best friends. I mean, I totally like Edie, but Laramie and I have *history*. And now she's friends with Nicolette and Gavin and those people. Everyone likes Laramie."

"Well, I know." She pauses. "But that doesn't mean she's not also threatened by your new friend across the street."

"You really think so?"

"I think it's highly plausible," she says.

I feel so much better than when I walked in here, and it hasn't even been five minutes. I don't want Laramie to be jealous of Edie, but I also like knowing maybe there's a reason she's been acting so different lately.

"Thanks, Denise." I stand to go back to my room so I can get in a few journal entries before bed. But then I remember something she just said: *I don't know all the facts*... "Can I ask you something?"

"Of course."

"If you're having trouble finding something for a story... research... what do you do?"

"Oh," she says, surprised. "Well, we are living in the golden age of information, so it's easier to find people and facts now than it's ever been. But with so much at our fingertips, there's also a lot of room for incorrect information. What are you trying to find?"

Ugh. I should have thought of what to say before I started asking questions. I'm not ready to tell anyone about the journals. They still belong to Edie and me for now. I don't want anyone else knowing Constance's story. Not until we figure out who she is.

"Um, just a school paper."

Denise raises her eyebrows. "Research papers in seventh grade? Schools really have come a long way."

"It's more like a profile." I feel bad lying to Denise, but I'd feel worse if I told her about Constance before Edie and I were ready.

"When I can't find something online, my next stop is usually the library."

I wrinkle my nose. "The library?" I don't want to spend a bunch of time looking through old, dusty books that may or may not help. And how would I even know where to start? As far as I know, cities don't have yearbooks of every person who ever lived there.

"I know, I know—so antiquated, right?" Denise laughs. "But the library is your best bet. They have reference books that can't be checked out, and micro-film."

"Microfilm?" I've never even heard that word.

"It's a way of viewing archives of newspapers, newsletters, government documents...maybe town directories." My ears perk up. A town directory sounds a lot like a yearbook. "I haven't been to the library here, but it looks nice from the outside. It might be worth going up there to see if they can help you find what you're looking for."

I don't know if it will be helpful. I picture Edie and me combing through stacks of huge, heavy old books and turning up nothing. But I guess it can't hurt. Because we're pretty stuck right now when it comes to Constance.

December 23, 1955

Mrs. Hansen found my <u>Sun-Reporters</u>.

She knows.

And now, two days before Christmas, I have nowhere to sleep.

Lord have mercy on me.

Love, Constance

RUBBER DUCKY

"WHY ARE YOU SO QUIET?" EDIE ASKS THE NEXT afternoon.

It's Thursday after school, and we're on our way to the library. I know I've been quiet all day, but I couldn't get the whole thing with Laramie out of my head. Every time I look at Edie, I remember what she said about her.

The funny thing is that the more I'm around Edie, the less I think about what she's wearing. I barely even notice her black lipstick anymore. She'd look stranger without it. And I like having a friend who's interested in different things than me. She talks about New York a lot, but when I think about leaving Ewing Beach, my throat gets tight. I'd probably talk about it all the time, too, if I ever had to move.

"Just tired," I say. "We got home kind of late after the gallery show."

She sighs, her boots clomping a distinct rhythm on the sidewalk. "I used to go to the studio sometimes with my dad when he was recording with artists. It was so amazing, seeing him work. He's still my dad, but, like, a totally different person when he's behind the boards."

If I could go back in time, I think I'd ask Edie to go with me to the show instead of Laramie.

"Ooh!" she says, her eyes getting huge. "I almost forgot to tell you—my dad is coming to visit next weekend!"

"Seriously?"

"Yeah, he's coming all the way to Ewing Beach, and Mom is going to let him stay in one of the rooms at the B&B." Edie is beaming. I think she's more excited than I've ever seen her. "I can't wait for you to meet him. You'll love him. Everybody loves him."

The library is located in a craftsman-style house that looks a lot like Edie's, only it's smaller and taupe-colored with mint-green trim and a wrap-around porch. There's a slot on the front for book returns, and a wreath made of yellowed book pages hangs on the front door above the EWING BEACH PUBLIC LIBRARY sign.

The bell jingles as we step inside and I think of the mooing cow at Coleman Creamery. I haven't been since school started. I think about Leif and wonder if he's giving Nicolette McKee free ice cream now instead of me.

"Good afternoon, girls," says Mrs. Palmer. She's the head librarian, and Mrs. Harris's daughter. I saw her at the B&B a few times before Edie moved in, when all of Mrs. Harris's kids were helping clean out her things. I've always thought she was pretty, with curly dark hair she wears in an angular bob and freckles sprinkled across her nose.

"Hi, Mrs. Palmer," I say with a smile.

She returns it as she steps away from her computer and leans her elbows on the counter. "It's good to see you, Alberta. How have you been?"

"Good," I say. "School is really busy this year, though."

"Are you in sixth grade now?"

I shake my head. "Seventh." Then I see her eyes warmly taking in Edie, so I say, "This is Edie. She and her mom bought the B&B."

Mrs. Palmer's eyebrows rise. "Of course. It's nice to meet you, Edie. I hope you're enjoying the bed and breakfast. My mother loved it very much."

"We love it, too," Edie says in the polite voice I've only heard her use with adults. "I live in the attic."

"Oh!" Mrs. Palmer seems surprised, but gives a quick nod and another smile. "Well, let me know if you girls need help with anything, okay?"

We head to a table as far from the front desk as possible so we can talk without anyone overhearing us. A few people are huddled up behind the line of public computers, and out of the corner of my eye, I see others browsing the stacks. Thankfully, no one from school is here, and no one even looks up as we sit down across from each other.

Edie sets down her bag and gasps.

I follow her eyes to the table two down from us, where a plump tortoiseshell cat is curled on top, snoozing away. "That's Jordan. She lives here."

Edie jumps up and bounds over to her, pausing with her hand above Jordan's head. "Is she friendly?"

"Yeah, just don't touch her stomach."

"That's totally like my cat, Arnold," Edie says. "He would try to claw your face off if you even went near it." Then she leans down next to Jordan, cooing, "And you are so pretty, just like Arnold."

Jordan's ears perk up and her green eyes flick open at the sound of Edie's voice. Then, as Edie gently strokes her head, her eyes slowly close into contented slits. I can hear her purring all the way over here.

"I've literally never met a cat who doesn't like me," Edie says, returning to the table after several minutes of loving on Jordan.

I pull out the list of facts we have about Constance and place it on the table between us. Edie adds the photograph. We both stare at it.

"I have a theory," I say in a low voice.

"Please do enlighten us, Ms. Freeman-Price," Edie says, and we both giggle. It's a perfect imitation of our history teacher, Ms. Gillingham.

"Constance was black."

Edie's eyes widen to approximately the size of dinner plates.

"She never comes out and says it in the journals I have," I continue. "At least not so far. But she's really interested in what's happening to black people. And she seems really…affected by it. She also has this huge secret that she's worried about everyone finding out."

Edie runs her fingers along the edge of the picture. "You really think this woman is black?"

I stare at Constance's sweet, open face. No, she doesn't look like any black people I know. Not even light-skinned black people. But I've seen pictures of people who passed for white, and they don't look a whole lot different from Constance.

"I do," I say to Edie.

"Well, she doesn't sign her full name in the journals I have." Edie stares down at the list as if it has all the answers. And I think it does, maybe. Only it's more like a puzzle now. One that's missing a few pieces. "And she keeps saying she's not going to mess up again."

"See? She said the man she knew back in Alabama probably would've been part of the bus boycotts. But black people were the ones boycotting, so he had to be black, right?"

"Or maybe she just had a black boyfriend."

I shake my head. "I don't think that was so easy back then, especially in the South. She got kicked out of her boardinghouse in San Francisco because she said the woman who ran it *knows*." I pull out the 1955 journal, flip to the last page, and slide it toward Edie. "And this is her last one from that year."

December 24, 1955

Mrs. Graham knows now, as well.

I had no other choice but to tell her I'd been pushed out of my room and had no place to go. When she asked why, I burst into tears, so exhausted by the last couple of days that I couldn't dredge up the energy for a lie.

She stood up from the table and began pacing across the kitchen. For a moment, she stopped by the telephone and I thought, perhaps, that she was going to call the police on me. Or perhaps she wanted to call Mr. Graham and ask him what to do. Then she stood by the sink for several minutes, wringing her hands as she stared out the window at nothing.

Finally, she sat back down across from me and said, "Constance, you know how much we appreciate you, but I'm afraid we can no longer employ you in our home."

"Please, Mrs. Graham. I have nowhere to go."

She looked down at the table as she said, "Mr. Graham and I are sympathetic to the struggles of your people. We truly are. But how would it look if we had a Negro house girl? Well, we'd be no better than the people from where you came."

"But no one has to know. You didn't, did you?" I stared at her until she met my eye.

"No, Constance, I didn't."

Somehow, that was a relief. Before she'd slammed the door at my back, Mrs. Hansen had snarled that she knew there was always something off about me.

I wondered who else knew. Patricia? Perhaps. Though I don't take her to be that perceptive. Most of our discussions center on parties and the young men we might meet at them and the clothes we would wear to impress them. Well, that <u>she</u> would wear. I've never gone to one of the gatherings or dances she's invited me to. I've taken my chances with a few people, but what if I fall in love? What if I had children and they turned out darker than me? My skin burned at the thought of Sanford. Was he thinking of loving other people, too? Of starting a family with another woman?

"But, Constance," Mrs. Graham said, "I'm afraid I can no longer trust you since you haven't been truthful with us. If you've lied about this, what else will you lie about?"

I felt so very low after that statement, I could no longer look her in the eye.

But she is giving me a place to stay through the new year. And she has promised she won't tell Mr. Graham or the children until I'm long gone.

"Can I give you some advice, Constance?"

I nodded as tears dripped down my cheeks.

Her voice was the kindest I've ever heard it as she said, "Maybe this is a sign that it's time to return home. Things are getting better down there every day. And I'm sure your family misses you very much."

I wiped the tears from my face before I looked at her again. "With all due respect, Mrs. Graham, if things were getting better I would never have felt the need to come so far and do what I did."

She said nothing. We sat silently across from each other until the telephone rang. It was Mrs. Ogden, confirming the Grahams would be at the Christmas Eve service that evening.

Love, Constance

Edie looks up at me, blinking rapidly. I think maybe she's trying to hold back tears. "This is so sad, Alberta. She was definitely passing for white."

We sit with that for a few moments. As hard as it is to be black in a town where not very many people look like me or understand what it is to be me, I can't imagine pretending to be white.

"It seems like it would be so much harder . . . pretending," Edie says quietly, as if she's read my mind.

"I don't know," I say. "Things were different back then. Especially in the South. Like she said, it was bad enough for her to lie about who she was."

She shakes her head. "I don't think I could do it."

"You wouldn't have to."

"What do you mean?" Edie says, frowning.

"You're light skinned."

"Not light enough to pass for white. And my dad always says I got the Whitman nose," she says. "I've never seen a white person with this kind of nose."

"Yeah, but things were different for light-skinned people back then." I pause. "Dad and Elliott say they're different today, too."

A stubborn look deposits itself on Edie's face, and I think maybe she's mad at me. Maybe I shouldn't have said anything.

Then she mumbles, "Craig used to say that all the time. He's dark, like my mom. My dad's skin is about your shade. I'm the lightest one in the family."

"Is that weird?"

Her voice is soft when she says, "Sometimes. People used to think I was Dominican. They'd look surprised when they'd see us all together."

I've always noticed when people stare at my dads and me, trying to figure out how we fit together, but it's never been because of the difference in our skin tones, which isn't a very big difference at all. I'm not light skinned. I'm not dark, either, but I'm a darker brown than Edie. No one would ever guess I'm any-thing but black.

Edie clears her throat. "I'm just saying, if Constance was light enough that she could pass for white but still had to leave the South, it sounds like it was pretty bad for anyone who wasn't actually white."

"Does she talk about passing in the journals you have?"

"No. Just her job at the department store, and the friends she's making." Edie pauses. "She seemed really happy in Santa Barbara. Maybe we should start looking for things about her life there?"

I glance at Mrs. Palmer, who's organizing books on a metal cart at the front of the library. "Denise said there's something called microfilm that we can use to look up stuff. Maybe we can find any Constances listed in Santa Barbara. Or an old town directory... or maybe something about the department store."

"Good idea," Edie says. "And we need to get to the end of these journals, stat."

"How many more are there?" The pile seemed endless when Edie first presented them to me.

"A lot. But we can skip ahead, right? I mean, she has to have some connection to Ewing Beach.

Otherwise, why were they all in my attic?" I look at Mrs. Palmer again, but before I can even say anything, Edie shakes her head. "No. We can't ask her. What if she makes us give them all to her?"

"She wouldn't do that. Mrs. Palmer is really sweet."

But part of me is worried about that, too. We did find them in her mother's old house. Maybe she and her sister and brother meant to take them but forgot about the box when they were moving out Mrs. Harris's personal things. I know they're not mine, but the more time we spend reading Constance's journals and turning the same pages that she touched and wrote on, the more attached to her I feel.

"Well, we can't use the microfilm if we don't ask her about it," I say. "She won't know exactly why we need to use it."

Edie still looks skeptical, but she follows me up to the front.

"Mrs. Palmer, we need some help," I say, trying not to sound as nervous as I feel. "Can we use microfilm to look up some really old stuff?"

She cocks her head to the side. "Are they teaching you about *microfilm* in school now?"

"No, our...family friend told me. She's a journalist, and she said it might help us find something for papers we're writing."

"Well, I can do my best to help, but it might take me a couple of days to pull up what you need," she says. "Hold on a second."

She gets a piece of paper and jots down everything we tell her: Santa Barbara, 1956, Schiff's Department Store, Betty Graham. I watch her face closely when I tell her the name Constance. Next to me, I feel Edie holding her breath. We're both worried Mrs. Palmer is going to recognize the information from the journals and tell us it's none of our business. Maybe she'll shut this whole thing down before we've even really started.

But she is completely professional as she takes the notes in neat, blocky handwriting. Edie has a couple of more names for her from the Santa Barbara journals she's read.

"How soon do you need the information?" Mrs. Palmer asks when she's done.

"Um, it's kind of a long-term project," I reply.

"But the sooner we can start, the better," Edie says quickly.

"Understood. Okay if I give you a call when I have everything set up? I'm not sure how much we have in the Ewing Beach archives, and I might need to contact some other local libraries for help."

"Totally okay with us," I say, and give her my number.

"You'll hear from me soon." She slides the paper onto her computer keyboard and smiles at us again. "It's nice to see girls your age taking an interest in history. Even if it is for a project. Most people these days think if it doesn't exist on the internet, it didn't happen."

Edie and I pack up our things and say good-bye to Mrs. Palmer before we leave.

As we walk along Ewing Street toward home, Edie says, "I have to tell you something."

I look at her curiously, wondering if there's some detail she didn't mention about Constance. Something she didn't want to say in front of Mrs. Palmer.

But she pauses and says, "Today...Rashawn gave me something."

"Rashawn Carlson?"

"Yeah...."

I wait for her to go on, but instead, I watch Edie's

tawny skin flush from the neck up. Finally, she stops next to a bench in front of the thrift store. She plops her backpack down, unzips it, and digs deep into the bottom. I'm definitely not expecting what she pulls out: a black rubber ducky.

I giggle as she hands it to me. "Where'd you get this?"

"From *Rashawn*."

"Why would he give you this?"

Her face looks like it's on fire. "He won it at the bottle toss...during Beach Night."

"But why would he give it to you?" I ask, frowning.

"He said he watched us playing so much that night. He felt bad that we never won anything. So... he won and chose this because he thought I'd like it."

"But Beach Night was almost a week ago. Why did he wait so long to give it to you?"

Edie shrugs. "Maybe he was nervous?"

I feel hot, too. Embarrassed.

"It's weird, right?" she says in a small voice. "I barely know him."

I turn the ducky over in my hand. Rashawn knows Edie well enough to know she'd like a jet-black rubber ducky better than a regular old yellow one.

It's pretty cute, but I don't really want to hold it anymore. I give it back to Edie.

"What should I do with it?" she asks, dropping it into her bag. She zips it up but doesn't put it back on her shoulders. A couple of seconds later, she sits on the bench and places the backpack on her lap.

I sit down next to her. "Keep it, I guess."

"But what if he thinks it means something?"

"I think it *does* mean something, Edie. He likes you."

She scrunches her nose. "But why? We've barely talked."

"I don't know...but isn't it kind of cool that someone likes you?"

"I guess. Except now do I have to like him back?"

I look at her. "Why would you have to do that?"

"It's..." She trails off, staring at the toes of her boots. "It's just that it's different here, right? Like, there are only two black guys at our school."

"So?"

"So...I like black guys, but is it weird if I don't like *him*? The ducky is sweet. And...I mean, he is kind of cute. But I just...I don't really feel that way about him."

"I totally get it," I say, rolling my eyes. "Rashawn's family just moved here last year, and everyone kept asking if I had a crush on him. It was super annoying. They never asked me about anyone else...just him."

Edie nods. "Because he's black. It's so weird. Brooklyn is, like, a huge melting pot. Nobody thinks you should have a crush on someone just because they're black or white or Puerto Rican or whatever." She pauses. "What do I do? I don't want to be rude, but..."

But she doesn't like him like that.

"Are you allowed to date?"

"Uh, no," she says, laughing. "My mom says I'm trying to grow up too fast with the coffee and lipstick. So I guess it doesn't matter anyway."

"Yeah, just tell him that," I say breezily. Like it's the easiest thing in the world. Or like I would know anything about talking to someone who likes me like *that*.

Edie turns to me. "Do *you* like anyone?"

I shrug. "No, not really."

"Not really or not at all?" she asks, raising her eyebrow like she's a sleuth in the mystery that is Alberta Freeman-Price.

But that part of me isn't interesting enough to be

a mystery. I've had crushes; my first one was Leif, even though I denied it every time Laramie brought up the way I got giggly and shy around him. I guess I stopped crushing on him last year sometime. He's still cute, but I noticed that I wasn't getting that strange, butterfly-flapping feeling in my stomach when I was around him. After Leif, I decided I liked a guy named Tate, who always smiled and said, "Hi, Alberta"— not just hi—when he saw me, until Laramie said she had it on good authority that Tate doesn't like girls. I guess I'm crushless at the moment.

"Not at all."

"Not even *Oliver*?"

"What? No!" I meet her grin with a suspicious stare. "Why?"

"I don't know. You guys are cool with each other."

"We're friends...and we know each other from surfing. But I don't like Oliver."

To be honest, I hadn't thought about it. Oliver is cute enough, and we do get along, but I've never thought about holding hands or kissing him or anything like that.

She shrugs. "That's fair. I don't like anyone here, either. Yet."

As we leave the bench and keep walking, Edie changes the subject to the collage project we started in art today. But I can't stop thinking about all the guys at Ewing Beach Middle School, trying to figure out if there's anyone I could have a crush on. I'd never admit this to anyone, but I even run over the list of sixth-grade boys who aren't completely repulsive. I come up with no one.

Really, though, I can't stop thinking about that rubber ducky. Rashawn is nice, but I've never liked him as more than friends. So I wish it didn't bother me so much that he likes Edie in a way he's never liked me.

SURF'S UP

Saturday morning, Elliott drives me to the community center, where I'm supposed to meet Irene and the rest of the kids so we can all go to the festival together.

I look over at Elliott. He keeps rubbing his eyes behind his glasses and yawning, which makes me yawn. It's earlier than either of us like to be up on a Saturday, but they didn't want me to have to leave my bike at the community center or walk there alone.

"Just imagine next year," I say wistfully as I fiddle with the radio dial. "You, Dad, and me will be on our way to Pismo so you can watch *me* compete."

"If that's what you want, I hope we will be, Al," he says stopping at a light.

"Why wouldn't it be what I want?"

"Well, sometimes things change. Our priorities. Interests."

"I'm *always* going to want to surf, Elliott," I say, folding my arms in front of me.

"I don't doubt that. I am curious why you're so interested in competing."

"Because it *proves* something. That I'm good enough to be out there with everyone else." Nobody will even know how good I am if I'm sitting on the sidelines.

"We already know you're good enough," Elliott says. "The best at camp, right?"

"Yes, but that's only what Irene said. Everyone gets a trophy, so there's no proof."

Elliott tilts his head at me. "But if you know it in your heart, and your instructor said that's what she thinks, too, why do you need a trophy to prove it?"

I look down at my lap. "Nicolette told me Irene was only saying that to make me feel better. About being different."

The light turns green, but Elliott takes a few

moments to go. He's just staring at a point over my shoulder. For so long that a car finally honks at him to get moving. And it takes a lot for people to honk at anyone in Ewing Beach.

"She said that to you?" he asks, finally putting his foot on the gas.

"Yeah... right after Irene walked away."

Elliott looks mad. And he usually tries not to get angry in front of me, so this must be a big deal to him. "I'm sorry, Al. She should never have said anything like that to you. She shouldn't even *think* like that, but..." He trails off, shaking his head.

Maybe *I'm* the one who shouldn't have mentioned anything. I don't want to make Elliott angry, especially not so early in the morning. Neither of us says anything else the rest of the way.

Irene is standing outside the community center next to a giant white conversion van. I'm relieved not to see any surfboards sitting on top of it or sticking out of the back. At least I'm not the only one who won't be competing today.

Elliott gives me a hug, carefully holding his travel mug, before I get out of the car. "I'm sorry you have to put up with ridiculous things like that, Al," he says into my dreads. "Ridiculous people. You know what she said isn't true, right?"

I nod as we pull away and start to open the door.

"Al?"

I look back at Elliott, whose face is full of concern. "I really want to know you hear me when I say Irene didn't tell you that because you're black. She told you that because it's the truth. Okay?"

"I hear you," I say softly. I'm a little embarrassed at how serious he's being. "Thanks, Elliott."

"And next year is your year to get out there and compete."

I smile at him and kiss his cheek before I get out of the car.

"Hey, Alberta," Irene says, waving as I walk up. Her hair is pulled back in its usual ponytail, the red strands gleaming like copper in the sun. "There are pastries and juice inside if you haven't eaten breakfast. We're taking off in about fifteen minutes."

"Fifteen minutes on the dot," says Jed, who's sitting in the front passenger seat, his legs hanging out of the open door. He gives me a lazy smile.

When I get inside the community center, I look around to see who's here. Most of the kids are a couple of years younger than me. Actually, there doesn't seem to be anyone my age here. I think Corey is my best hope. She's two years older, but she's never been rude to me. And she's looking around, too, like she's desperate to find someone her age.

I decide to get something to eat before I go talk to her. Just as I'm grabbing an almond croissant, someone behind me says, "Hey, Alberta."

Oliver is standing behind me with a cup of orange juice.

"Hey." I rip off a piece of croissant and stuff it in my mouth. Ever since Edie asked if I have a crush on Oliver, it's the first thing I think of when I see him. I felt like I was going to disappear in a ball of flames when I saw him yesterday at school, like he'd somehow know we'd been talking about him.

"No Laramie this year?" he asks, looking closely at the boxes of pastries. He finally settles on a jelly doughnut.

I try not to frown. "She's not in surf camp."

"Duh. But she always goes to watch her brother, right? Is she going up to Pismo with her family?"

"No, she's going to Nicolette's birthday party."

Oliver takes a huge bite of his doughnut, barely catching the red jelly before it drips onto his shirt. And he gets powdered sugar everywhere. But at least he doesn't talk with his mouth full, like Fletcher. "Why is she hanging out with eighth graders all the time now?"

"I don't know," I say. And I don't want to talk about it, so I change the subject. "Hey, would your parents let you compete?"

He licks a drop of jelly from the side of his finger. "I don't want to compete. I just like surfing."

"But if you *wanted* to, would they let you?"

"I don't know." Oliver shrugs. "I guess. My parents don't really care about surfing. Just soccer. My dad, mostly."

"Do they make you play?" Oliver is on the team, and he's supposed to be pretty good, but I've never seen one of his games.

"No, I like it. But my dad played, growing up. He still plays in leagues. And my abuelo played in Club América, back in Mexico City. So it's kind of a family thing." He looks at me, wiping powdered sugar from his chin. "Why? You wanna compete?"

"Yeah, but my dads won't let me until I turn thirteen."

He shrugs. "So you can do it next year, right? That's not so far off."

"Ugh," I say, walking away from him to the jugs of juice on the other side of the table.

"Hey, what's wrong?"

"You sound *exactly* like my dads."

The beach is already bursting with surfers and spectators by the time Jed lets us out with Irene and goes to park the van. Booths selling everything from tacos to surf gear to beer are set up along the boardwalk, leading down to the pier.

Everywhere I look, people are in wet suits and rash guards, holding their boards. My arms ache to hold my own, feeling the empty space beneath them. I'm starting to wonder if I should have come at all, because I can't help feeling jealous no matter where I glance.

We find a space big enough for all eight of us and spread out beach blankets on the sand. I sit next to

Oliver, who seems scared to say anything after I got annoyed with him. Irene is on my other side, already reapplying sunscreen to her face.

The groms are up first, which is what they call little kids who surf. Leif used to call me that when he first met me. In this contest, it's kids ten and under. These kids are *really* good, riding waves that would have terrified me at that age. A few of them even pull off some tricks that make everyone on the beach clap and cheer.

"Did you ever think about going pro?" I ask Irene when the next age group is up. Girls, eleven to seventeen. The group I'd be competing in.

She glances around us, as if to see if anyone is listening. Then she leans her head close to mine. "Between you and me, yes."

"But why is it a secret? I bet you were good enough."

Irene has shown us videos of her surfing when she was a teenager. Maybe so we'd believe she knew what she was talking about as she coached us.

"Because I wasn't good enough," she says with a sigh. "Almost, but... the truth is, I didn't have the discipline to go as far as I could have. I was more interested in parties and boys. And I didn't want to get up early on the weekends to practice." She looks at me and shakes her head. "Silly, huh?"

"But it's not too late, is it?"

Irene gives me a wry smile. "I'm afraid so. But, also, it was different for young women back then. Nobody really encouraged us to do anything with our talent. It was seen as more of a hobby rather than a sport we wanted to compete in, too. Of course women surfers have been around as long as the sport has, but it's only been in the last couple of decades or so that we've been given our due."

"My dads think I'm still too young to enter a contest," I say, digging the toe of my sneaker into the sand.

"I know."

I look at her. "You do?"

"I asked Kadeem about it a few months ago. I thought you'd be perfect for this competition, and I was sure of it after the way you performed at camp this summer."

"But he said no." I sigh.

"He said they'd feel more comfortable if you took another year before you started to compete. That they just want you to have fun with it for now."

"Yeah, that's exactly what they tell me," I mumble. "But...you really think I'm good enough, Irene?"

"You know I do," she says, nudging me with her elbow.

"No, I mean...seriously? You wouldn't just say that to make me feel better?"

She fixes her eyes on me sternly. "Have you ever known me to lie?"

"No, I just...I wouldn't want you to say that because I'm...different, or whatever."

"Different?" She frowns. "I know a good surfer when I see one, Alberta. Skin color has nothing to do with it. I'll always be honest with you, okay?"

"Okay." I draw my knees up to my chest and rest my chin on them, wrapping my arms around myself so she won't see my huge, relieved smile.

I walk down to the edge of the sand when Leif is up.

When he's in the water, it's hard to believe he's

the same guy who dirties up the kitchen with his ridiculous culinary creations and wears a silly paper hat while he's scooping ice cream. He gets this super-focused face where he squints his eyes and presses his lips together into a thin line. And he moves around on the board like he's never met a wave that doesn't like him.

Some of his friends from school are here, cheering him on a few feet away from me. I scan the crowd behind me, looking for his and Laramie's mother. She's standing next to a blanket, wearing sunglasses and a wide-brimmed hat as she watches Leif surf. It's weird not to be standing next to her. I turn around before she can see me.

Leif is amazing on the board, pulling a couple of tricks I hope to perfect someday, like a round-house cutback so beautiful it makes my breath catch in my throat. He can't stop grinning as he paddles back in. His friends crowd around him, clapping him on the shoulder and giving him good-natured punches in the arm as droplets of water drip down his wet suit. He starts to walk away, then sees me and stops.

"Alberta, hey! I didn't know you were coming," he says, his teeth shining in the sun.

"I wouldn't miss it!"

"Oh, I thought maybe you were at that party Laramie went to."

I shake my head. "I wasn't invited....But I'd rather be here, anyway. You were so, so good."

"Thanks, grom," he says, and it makes me smile even though I'm too old to be called that now. "Haven't seen you around in a while, Alberta. You know, I bet I can scrounge up a free scoop of butter pecan even if you drop by when my sister isn't there."

I want to know what Leif means by that. Does he know things have been weird between Laramie and me lately?

"Seventh grade has been keeping me pretty busy."

"I bet. That's when all the real homework starts. Who are you here with?"

"Just some people from surf camp." I gesture to where Irene, Oliver, and everyone else is sitting.

"That party Laramie went to must not be so great if you're here. Who wouldn't invite you?" he says, shaking his head. "Good seeing you, Alberta. Stop by Coleman anytime."

My skin warms from Leif's words. At least he still thinks I'm fun to hang out with.

He tucks his board under his arm and heads back to where Mrs. Mason is sitting, waving a damp hand as he leaves.

I wish I could see into the future. Will I be here next year—competing? And will Laramie come to see me if I am?

BFF

When I get home from Pismo, Laramie is sitting in the kitchen with Dad and Denise, watching them make dinner.

"What are you doing here?" I ask, then clap my hand over my mouth. It's never been strange to see Laramie in my house...until now.

"I was at Nicolette's, so I thought I'd stop by." Her eyes meet my face briefly before going down to her hands.

Elliott drops his keys on the kitchen table and squeezes Laramie's shoulder before heading to the stove to investigate.

"Oh. Right." I stand across the room, looking at her. "How was the party?"

"Fine," she says quickly. "How was the competition? Mom texted to say Leif came in second in the boys' group."

"He was really good. He probably only missed first by, like, a couple of points."

Laramie finally looks at me again and nods. "Cool."

"Why don't you girls go hang out while we finish up dinner?" Denise says, looking over at us. She catches my eye before she asks, "Laramie, you're staying, right?"

"Um, I can." She glances at me. "If it's okay."

"Of course you're staying." I grab her hand to pull her up from the table. "We're going for a walk."

"We'll be ready to eat in thirty minutes, Alberta," Dad says over his shoulder. "Be back by then, please."

Laramie and I head out the front door, and I do my best not to look at Nicolette's. It's hard to believe Laramie was just there, not even a hundred steps from my house all afternoon. When we're a few houses down, she says, "Stephan McKee was *terrible* today. Like, I can't believe they even allowed him to be in the house. Rebekah was watching him, but he kept running down from the playroom to see what we were doing at the party. And when they lit the candles, he blew them out before Nicolette and grabbed a handful of cake before anyone could stop him."

I can't help it—I let out a laugh. "What did Nicolette do?"

"She was pretty mad." When I look over, a smile teases at the corner of Laramie's lips.

Somehow, that little anecdote makes me feel better about my best friend being at a party I wasn't invited to.

"I have to tell you something," she says after a few moments.

Oh no. Is she going to tell me she doesn't want to be best friends anymore?

"But you have to promise not to tell anyone else."

I give her a look. "Laramie. I'm your best friend."

At least I hope I still am.

"I know, but you—you can't tell Edie, okay?"

"I don't tell her *everything*."

"I don't know...you guys are together all the time now."

"Only as much as you're with Nicolette," I reply.

Laramie sighs. "Just don't tell anyone, okay?"

I cross my fingers over my heart. "Promise."

She taps the cat-shaped mailbox that sits at the end of the Garrisons' driveway. "I like someone." And then, before I can even take a guess, she whispers, "Gavin."

"Whoa." I stop right there on the sidewalk.

"Yeah." She stops, too, looking down the street at nothing. "Sometimes . . . I think he likes me back."

"But what about Nicolette?"

Her head turns sharply toward me. "What about her?"

"Well, you said you had to go with her to his party for moral support on Beach Night. And Edie asked if she liked him. . . ."

"And I never said she did," Laramie responds, frowning. Then the frown drops and she sighs. "Look, you can't tell anyone about this, Alberta."

"I already promised I wouldn't."

"I just had to tell someone. I felt like I would burst if I didn't."

Someone? Wasn't she planning to tell me anyway? Or is Nicolette the first person she goes to now?

"Well, what are you going to do about it? Tell him?" I look over at the yellow house across the street where Mr. Mortimer is standing on the porch watering his plants. He sees me watching and waves. I wave back.

"God, no," Laramie says, starting to walk again. Her long legs are moving so fast I have to hurry to catch up to her.

"So you're just going to keep it a secret forever?"

"I don't *know*, Alberta! I've never liked someone I was actually hanging out with." Her face is red as a lobster and she looks so frustrated she might cry.

"Well, he's dumber than I thought if he doesn't like you back," I say.

"Uh, thanks?"

"Sorry." I loop my arm through hers so we can walk at the same pace. "I just mean... you're really cool. And smart. And pretty. He should *definitely* like you back."

"Whatever. I don't think Gavin would go out with a seventh grader anyway," she says, waving her arm. As if the whole thing is just a silly confession she never should have shared.

"Yeah, but you're Laramie," I say with a smile.

She smiles back at me and squeezes my arm. "Thanks."

"For what?"

"For being my best friend."

INVISIBLE MAN

EDIE AND I GO BACK TO THE LIBRARY AFTER SCHOOL on Monday. Mrs. Palmer has something for us.

"I couldn't find as much as I would have liked," she says as she sets up the microfilm at a table behind the reference desk. "But it's better than nothing and might lead to more."

She shows us how to load the microfilm machine, how to adjust the slides, and how to save and print out anything we find.

"I hope it's helpful, girls," she says when we're all set up. "I'll be around the corner shelving if you need anything."

"I feel like we're so close to finding out who she was," Edie whispers at my side. I'm sitting in front of the computer screen. She said she felt more comfortable with me operating things.

"I hope so," I say as we look at the first slide.

We spend the next couple of hours reading different articles written about people and places in Santa Barbara. There are a few mentions of Schiff's Department Store, though a few of them are just ads for their beautiful, hand-tailored dresses. We find a marriage announcement for a Betty Graham, but she's not the one we're looking for. That Betty would still be living with her parents, wearing bunny costumes for Halloween.

I hold my breath when we get to the slides that mention a Constance. There's another marriage announcement, an obituary, a few listings in the city directory. Edie copies down all the names I whisper to her: Constance Charles, Constance Miller, Constance Ferguson.... Then she dashes off to the computer bank to look them up while I go through the slides again to make sure we didn't miss anything.

I close out of the last slide and push my chair up to the desk, then join Edie at the computer. She's leaning forward, her nose so close to the screen it's practically touching.

"How is it possible that none of these are the right Constance?" she mutters.

"Are you sure?"

"None of the information matches up. Most of them were born in California, or they're way too old or young to be her."

I sit down next to her as she finishes searching the list of Constances. She's right. None of them are the one we're looking for.

We both sit back in our seats, dejected.

"Now what?"

"Well, we still need to read the rest of the journals," I say slowly. "The later ones."

"I'm so tired of reading the journals," Edie moans. "No offense, but they're really depressing."

"I know," I say. "But I want to find out who she is. And how she knew Mrs. Harris."

Edie and I pack up our things, stopping to say thank you to Mrs. Palmer.

"I'm sorry you didn't find what you were looking for," she says. I guess it's pretty obvious by the looks on our faces. "But I'm here almost every day, so let me know if you girls think of anything else I can help you with before your project is due, okay?"

She goes back to typing something on her computer, smiling a good-bye as we walk out the door.

"Mom?" Edie calls when we step into the B&B.

"Back here in the library!"

The room is piled with books and smells like dust and—Denise is here. She's poring over an ancient-looking book while Ms. Whitman sits cross-legged on the floor, running a rag and furniture polish over the bottom shelf of a built-in bookcase.

"How was school?" Denise asks, smiling.

I hesitate and then, after a moment, I walk over to give her a hug. She wraps me into her arms, the fabric of her orange caftan soft against my cheek.

"Good," Edie says. She pauses, and I wonder if she's going to tell them about the journals. We might be able to figure out who Constance is faster than we can alone, but I still hope she doesn't. I like it being our secret. "I'm starving, Mom. Can we get a snack?"

"Of course. Denise, are you hungry, too?"

Denise rubs her belly with one hand. "We could eat."

Ms. Whitman stands, brushing her palms on her jeans. "Denise was nice enough to come over and help me try to get this library organized. Mrs. Harris's taste was . . . a little eclectic."

"I just don't understand why a woman in this town had so many copies of *Invisible Man*," Denise says, shrugging. Her arm is still around me and it feels cozy with her belly pressing against me on the other side.

Edie and her mother have already headed to the kitchen when Denise gasps and says, "Oh!"

I jump away from her, worried I've hurt her or the baby somehow. But she's grinning, and then, as she looks at me, Denise takes my hand and holds it to her stomach. Her belly feels like a basketball. It's so perfectly round, it's hard to believe there's a baby growing inside.

"Oh!" I say, too. I felt a thump where she placed my hand.

"That's the baby kicking."

My mouth drops open and I hold my breath,

hoping I'll get to feel it again. Just when I think the baby is going to be shy, there's a little thump again in the same place. "Wow."

"Pretty cool, huh? I think the baby likes Tim's voice, so I hold the phone up to my stomach whenever he calls so they can talk. Maybe the baby likes your voice, too."

No matter how many times I tell myself it's true, I can't believe I was the baby in there kicking Denise once.

I look around as we follow them to the kitchen. Ms. Whitman has been working hard on the bed and breakfast. They're all small changes, but they look good. She re-covered the chairs in the sitting area to a soft gray fabric with pink pillows. She's also switched out some of the art from the watercolor prints of flowers and meadows that Mrs. Harris had. The new pieces are photographs and paintings of the ocean, boardwalks, and beach scenes.

Ms. Whitman sets out hummus, warm pita bread, and some olives and cheese. Just before she sits down, her phone rings. She takes a look at the screen, frowns, and says, "I'm so sorry, but I need to take this. Edie, can you get everyone drinks?"

Her brows are still furrowed when she comes back a few minutes later, phone in hand. Edie sucks on an olive pit, staring at her mom. "What's wrong?"

"Nothing, honey. We'll talk about it later."

Now Edie's frowning. She spits out the pit and drops it into the tiny bowl on the table. "Did something happen? Is Craig okay?"

Ms. Whitman's eyes slide over to Denise and me. "We have guests, sweetie."

"I'm just going to tell Alberta later, anyway."

Her mother sighs. "That was your father. He's going to call you later, but he wanted to let me know he won't be able to make it this weekend."

Edie's entire body slumps. I can't tell if she's crying. Her hair falls in front of her face like a black sheet as she looks down at her lap.

"He's so sorry, Edie. He just couldn't make it work around a business trip he has in London. But he's going to call and figure out a good time to come soon, okay?"

I don't want to stare at Edie while she's upset, but I can't help it. She hasn't moved. I look at Denise, who mouths, *We should go.*

Ms. Whitman stands behind Edie, rubbing her

back. "It's going to be okay, sweetie," she murmurs. "You'll see him soon."

Denise and I quietly get up from the table and thank Ms. Whitman for the snack.

"I'll talk to you later, Edie," I say before we walk out of the kitchen. It doesn't feel good enough, but I'm not sure what else to say. She's still not looking at anyone.

Denise and I get to the front door before we hear Edie choking out a sob.

GUMBOTTOM

I crack open another journal before bed. This one is from 1956, and Constance is still loving Santa Barbara. I'm about to close it for the evening when I turn the page in the middle of the March entries and find a black-and-white photograph.

I gasp. Edie found the last picture, and I didn't expect to come across another one. I'm even more surprised to see it's a picture of a woman who's not Constance. This one was taken from far away, and it's of a tall, dark-skinned woman standing next to a pickup truck. I've only seen trucks like this in super-old pictures, just like this one. The woman is squinting into the sun, her hand resting on the side of the truck. Instead of a big smile, like Constance, her lips are pressed into a thin, straight line.

I wish I could see her face better, but it's blurry, even when I hold it close to my eyes. I turn it over, where it says *Juanita McCrimmons, Gumbottom, 1954.* The same year as the photo of Constance. Hers seemed like a professional picture, but this one looks like a shot taken by someone the woman knows.

I grab my phone to text Edie, but before I can pull up her name, someone knocks on my door. I quickly slide the picture and journal under the pillow behind me. They're not a secret, exactly, but it still feels like maybe Edie and I should have told someone we have these.

"Come in!"

Dad sticks his head in. "Almost time for lights out, sweetheart."

"I know. I'm just texting Edie."

He smiles. "You've become fast friends, huh?"

"Yeah.... Hey, Dad? Do you know anything about Edie's father?"

He twists his mouth to the side, thinking. "Probably not much more than you do. He works in music, and Calliope said it keeps him busy. Why?"

"Edie thinks she's never going to see him again."

"What? Oh, Alberta, I'm sure that's an exaggeration."

I scoop my knees up to my chest. "He was supposed to come visit this weekend, and now he's not."

"Well, sometimes plans change." Dad sighs. "We don't know what he has going on."

I want to say that's not fair, especially when someone is counting on you. He didn't see Edie when her mother told her. I don't think anyone has ever looked so sad.

"But I'm sorry for Edie," Dad says, making his way across the room to kiss the top of my head. "I know she's had to deal with a lot of change lately."

She's not the only one. But I just nod at my dad, give him a hug, and say good night. I'm sorry for Edie, too. And I hope she'll feel better in the morning, just like Dad and Elliott always say I will when I'm upset about something.

I slip the picture into my bag the next morning, making sure I tuck it between the pages of my notebook so it doesn't get creased or torn. I decided not to text

Edie about it after all. I figured she might cheer up a little when she sees it.

But when I go to the B&B after breakfast, Ms. Whitman opens the door with an apologetic smile. "Good morning, Alberta. I'm sorry, but Edie isn't feeling well today, so she's staying home."

I don't think Ms. Whitman is lying, but I'm pretty sure Edie not feeling well has everything to do with her dad and nothing to do with a cold or fever.

"Do you need a ride?" she asks, running a hand over her bandana. It's pink today.

"No, thank you. I'll ride my bike. Tell Edie I hope she feels better soon."

"I will, honey. She'll appreciate it. Have a good day, okay?"

I planned to wait for Edie before I looked up Juanita from the picture, but I have a feeling she doesn't care much about Constance's life right now. And maybe I can really cheer her up if I find out something about Juanita while she's home sick today.

"Where are you going?" Oliver asks when he passes me in the hallway before lunch. I'm walking in the opposite direction of the cafeteria, toward the library.

"I have to do some work for a class," I say, shifting impatiently.

He frowns. "During lunch?"

"I just...yeah. It's kind of important."

"All right, well, see you later," he says, waving his lunch sack in the air.

I slide into a seat behind the computer farthest from the library entrance and pull the picture from my notebook. I stare at it again and make a silent wish that there's something out there about Juanita McCrimmons. I have her first *and* last name. And what is Gumbottom? The name of a town?

I take a deep breath as I type in her name. A lot of hits come up in the search, but it's mostly random entries with all the individual words I typed in. Like someone named Lorna McCrimmons on Gumbottom Road. I scroll through the first page until I get to the bottom and—

"Oh my god!" I say out loud. So loud that the librarian looks over. And she's not as friendly as Mrs. Palmer. I shrink down in my seat as I click on the link. It's an online directory, with a few Juanita McCrimmonses, listed by location.

One lives in Alaska, and another one is in

Massachusetts. There's a Juanita McCrimmons who's in her fifties in Chicago, and another in her sixties who lives in Missouri. I do the math, and I'm pretty sure they're all too young to be the woman in the picture. I sigh and keep scrolling until—

I clap my hand over my mouth this time. Because there, right in front of me, is exactly who I think I'm looking for. A woman named Juanita McCrimmons. In *Gumbottom, Alabama*. But I deflate almost immediately. She died over ten years ago. And when I open a new tab and search for an obituary, nothing comes up.

I quickly scan the names under hers for people who might be related. Not all the last names match, but maybe they'll know something about this woman. Something about Constance. I scribble them down.

My stomach grumbles. I could take a break and still have time for lunch, but I want to finish what I started, so I begin looking up the new names. It's a short list, and not much comes up. More of the same online directory entries, and a few family-tree sites that don't lead to anything.

It seems like I've only been here a few minutes, but the next time I look at the clock, I have five minutes until lunch is over. Which is perfect timing, because I have one more name left. I type in *Rosemary McCrimmons* ... and she has a website!

Okay, so it's a link to a real estate agent's website, but it's still something. I click on it and press my palms against my knees as I wait for the page to load. A picture of a light-skinned black woman with short black hair pops up, followed by a bunch of boring stuff about houses.

But there's an e-mail address. And a phone number. And she's black, which means maybe she's related to Constance, too. I send the link to my e-mail and copy down her name and information in my notebook. I log out and stand up from the computer just as the bell rings, hugging the notebook to my chest.

BLEACHERS

THE NEXT DAY AT SCHOOL, EDIE IS SULLEN.

I can't think of any other word to describe her. We have an assembly during first period, and her boots clomp so loudly as we file into the gym the sound echoes off the walls like we're in military boot camp.

Ever since yesterday, the news about the picture and Juanita and Rosemary has been sitting on the tip of my tongue. I thought about e-mailing or calling Rosemary myself, but every time I reached for my phone, my heart started beating so fast that I set it right down again. I bet Edie wouldn't be nervous about calling her at all. I just can't find a good time to tell her.

Once we find seats on the bleachers with the rest of our class, she crosses her arms and stares straight ahead. She barely grunted a response when I said hi to her this morning. Now she's glaring straight ahead at nothing in particular.

I know she's not mad at me, but I feel bad that she's so upset. And I don't know what to say to make her feel better.

Oliver slides onto the empty space next to me. "Is that Laramie over there?" He's pointing to the wall of bleachers across the gym, where the eighth graders are gathered.

Everyone is supposed to be sitting with their grade, like we are, but Oliver is right. There's Laramie, perched at the top of the bleachers. Gavin is on one side of her, and Nicolette is sitting next to him.

"Man, she'd probably ditch our table if we had lunch with them, too," Fletcher says from the other side of Oliver. Of course he's chewing on something, and for once, I can't see what's rolling around in his mouth.

Edie doesn't even look over, but I channel her glare and turn it on the guys. Why are they paying attention to this stuff, anyway? They only started sitting with us this year.

I keep glancing at Laramie during the assembly, though. Even as Ms. Franklin stands at the front of the room in her seafoam-colored Crocs, recapping the first month of the school year and making announcements for October. I know every expression Laramie has ever made, and it's not hard to see she doesn't look happy... even though she's inches away from her crush.

Nicolette isn't talking to her at all. She just keeps flipping her hair back and forth, scanning the gym with a bored look on her face. Gavin leans over to Laramie every once in a while to say something in her ear. He always laughs and she smiles, but the smile fades as soon as he looks away. Every time he does this, Nicolette finds some reason to poke Gavin or nudge him with her shoulder, bringing his attention back to her.

After a while, I start trying to catch Laramie's eye, thinking maybe she'll crack a real smile if she sees me. Especially after she came over for dinner the other night, things seem almost back to normal with us. Almost. She never looks at me.

By the end of Ms. Franklin's announcements, Laramie is staring at her feet, tucking her curls behind her ears and looking at no one.

"What up, Wednesday Addams?"

Does Fletcher have a death wish? He hasn't called Edie that since the first day of school, and I don't know why he chose today of all days to do it again. I haven't seen her smile since we set foot in the building.

She doesn't even look at him now as she listlessly swirls a spoon through her yogurt cup. So, dumbo Fletcher says it louder.

"Hey, Wednesday."

"Quit it, Fletcher," I say in the sternest tone I can muster.

When Edie still doesn't say anything, he shrugs and looks at me. "What's wrong with her?"

"None of your business," I answer, because it sounds like something Edie would say, and she's clearly not speaking today unless she absolutely has to.

Across the table, Laramie is quiet, too. I wonder if it has something to do with Nicolette not talking to her during the assembly. Or Gavin sitting between them.

When Laramie gets up to toss her trash, I follow her, even though I'm not done with my lunch.

"Hey," I say, jogging to catch up to her with my tray in hand.

She looks over her shoulder. "Oh, hey."

"Are you okay?"

"I'm fine. Why?"

"You just seem...kind of quiet, I guess."

"I'm fine," she repeats in a firmer tone. A tone that means she wants me to drop it.

But I don't think best friends are supposed to just drop it.

"Is everything okay with you and Nicolette?"

She stops outside the doors to the cafeteria. "Um, yeah. Why wouldn't it be?"

"I saw you...sitting with her at the assembly."

"So?" Laramie is frowning now, but I keep talking.

"So, you looked really unhappy." I take a deep breath. "And it looked like Nicolette kept trying to get Gavin to talk to her every time he said something to you."

Something flashes across Laramie's face. Sadness? Relief that I noticed? Especially since I'm the only person she's told about her crush?

But then, a second later, the expression is replaced by a dark look. "Seriously, Alberta?"

I wince. Laramie has never looked at me like that. "What?"

"Are you *seriously* so jealous that I'm friends with Nicolette? You don't have to make things up, you know. Everything with Nicolette is fine. Everything is *fine*, okay?"

"I just..." What happened? It's like we never went on that walk at all. This definitely isn't the Laramie who confessed her crush to me and thanked me for being her best friend.

She whips around and stalks into the cafeteria, not even giving me time to finish my sentence.

"Have you had a chance to read any of the other journals?" I ask Edie on the walk home from school.

Maybe now is a good time to bring up Juanita.

"No offense, but I wasn't really in the mood to catch up on Constance's life when I'm never going to see my dad again."

"Oh." I pause. Maybe there'll never be a good time with the mood Edie has been in, so I forge ahead. "Well, I found something. Some*one* who might be able to tell us something about Constance."

She doesn't look as excited as I hoped she would, but she doesn't look *un*interested. I quickly tell her about all the things I found and stop to pull out my notebook. I show her the picture.

"Do you think this is her mom?" she asks, staring at the woman by the truck.

I shrug. "I don't know. But I think we should call this Rosemary woman. She might know something."

"Where does she live?"

"Atlanta," I say. "But she has the same last name. And she's black, too."

I hope she'll say we should go call her right now. And that she should be the one to call...because I think I might be too nervous to do it.

But Edie only nods, so I don't say anything else. I just match my steps to the beat of her boots thumping on the pavement.

I go inside the B&B with her so we can split up the rest of the later journals from the box. She may not be in the mood to read them, but I'm ready to get started on the rest of our research.

Ms. Whitman looks at us cautiously when she asks how school was, and I answer quickly so we don't have to deal with an awkward silence or grumble from Edie.

"Well," says Edie's mother, "I have some good news." Edie's eyebrows lift, but before she can say anything, Ms. Whitman holds up her hand. "No, I'm sorry, but your father still isn't coming this weekend."

Edie folds her arms across her chest.

"*But*. If it's all right with you, I was thinking we could have a little Halloween party here at the B&B."

For the first time today, I see Edie smile. And when we're on the stairs up to her bedroom, she says, "Should we call that woman in Atlanta?"

Edie doesn't look nearly as nervous as I was when I even *thought* about calling Rosemary McCrimmons, and she's actually putting her number into her phone.

"What are you going to say?" I ask before she pushes the call button.

Edie just shrugs and puts the phone on speaker.

"Rosemary McCrimmons," a warm voice says, picking up after the third ring.

Edie's face changes. I think it must be her grown-up face, because the voice she uses is definitely a grown-up voice.

"Hello, Rosemary? My name is Edith, and I'm calling to ask if you might be able to help me."

"Edith?" It sounds like she's shuffling some papers around on a desk. "Have we spoken before?"

"No, but my question is of a more personal nature," Edie says, sitting tall.

The shuffling stops. "Okaaaay. How can I help you?"

"I'm looking for someone who might know a Juanita McCrimmons. Or someone named Constance. From Gumbottom, Alabama."

I can practically hear Rosemary frowning through the phone. The warm voice is gone. "Who's asking?"

"My name is Edith," Edie repeats. She quickly adds, "Edith Minturn."

My eyes widen. I hope Rosemary doesn't know anything about Edie Sedgwick and all her names.

"And what is this regarding, Edith?" The woman's voice is getting slower the more she talks.

I coil and uncoil one of my locs around my finger. We never discussed what she'd say if she actually got Rosemary on the phone.

Edie hesitates for only a few seconds before she responds, "I've found some items that might belong to their family, and I'm trying to reach the proper contact."

There's a long pause on the other end. Edie raises her eyebrow at the phone, but she waits until Rosemary speaks again.

"Where did you find those names?"

"In the belongings."

"And where were the belongings found?"

"In California."

"You sound young."

"With all due respect, Ms. McCrimmons, I'm not sure what my age has to do with this," Edie says in an even more professional voice. "I'm simply trying to return items to their rightful owner."

There's silence again. Then Rosemary finally says, "Juanita was a distant cousin, and she's been gone for some time now, as far as I know. What was the other name?"

"Constance," Edie says.

And then we both hold our breath as we wait for her to respond. She clears her throat.

"I'm sorry, Edith, but I don't know that name. Now, if you'll excuse me, I need to get back to work."

"But what about the—"

The phone clicks and she's gone.

"Noooo," I moan, staring at Edie's cell.

She glares at it before she sets it on the rug.

"We were so close," I say. "Do you think she knows more than she's saying?"

Edie shakes her head. "No. I think maybe she was weirded out by some stranger calling and asking about her family. At least she told us about Juanita."

"I've already looked up Constance McCrimmons, and nothing came up." I sigh. "How can it be this hard to find out who someone was? We have pictures. And a whole *box* full of journals."

Edie bites her lip. "Maybe Constance really doesn't want to be found."

I'm starting to think Edie is right.

*Today is Sanford's birthday. Just like Christmas,
it's as if the day he was born is imprinted in my
brain forever. A day I can never forget.*

*It is also the day I feared my loose tongue
was the beginning of the end. I voluntarily told
my supervisor, May, about my background.*

*I hadn't planned to do so. I went to Schiff's,
like normal, and stowed my purse in the back
room. I drank a glass of water before my shift
began. And when May came in to retrieve her
cardigan and say hello, she must have seen
something in my eyes because she stopped and
asked me what was wrong.*

*"Nothing," I said two times, but when
it was apparent she would not take that for
an answer, I faltered. "It's the birthday of
someone I care about very much," I said after a
pause. "And I can't be with them."*

May raised a suggestive eyebrow. "Them?"

"May," I said, shaking my head.

*"My apologies, Constance." Her face turned
serious. "But am I right? Is this about a man?"*

It was hard to think of Sanford as a man. He was so young when we met in the schoolhouse—both of us were, at only seven years old. But it wasn't long before others started to act as if he were twice his age, treating him like a man but calling him "boy."

I nodded. "Yes. We...I haven't spoken to him since I left Alabama."

A tingle danced through my palms with that admission. I'd never even mentioned the South to anyone in San Francisco for fear of being found out. Mrs. Graham was right—I'd lied to her more than once. Upon our first meeting, in fact, when I told her I'd relocated from Chicago. Getting rid of my Southern accent had been easier than I'd imagined.

May tilted her head at me. "And you love him?"

"I care for him."

"Constance," she said with a soft smile, "I can see in your eyes that you love this man. Why don't you call him?"

I laughed out loud. "A long-distance call from me, out of the blue after more than a year? What would he think?" Not to mention that the cost of the call would eat up my wages for the week.

"It's worth a try," May encouraged.

"Not after how I left things between us."

Which is to say that I left without a proper good-bye. I wrote him a letter, similar to the one I left for Mama, Papa, and Henry. I said I knew he didn't want me to leave, but it was the only way I knew to live life. I told him that I loved him but even if he gave me the world, which I knew he'd try, I couldn't be happy with the life we'd be forced to live in Alabama.

"Constance, what happened?" May moved closer to me, putting her hand on my arm.

"I should really get out to the sales floor, May," I said, gesturing to the door behind her.

"Mary Ellen can handle the floor just fine for a few minutes. Besides, you're early. What's wrong, Constance?"

I blame what happened next on the fact that her hand felt so comforting and I was starved for human touch. So much that I even missed the hugs of the Graham children when they deemed something I'd done for them particularly nice. Or perhaps I was just tired. Of hiding my true self, of waiting to be discovered and chastised and kicked out of the second new life I'd made.

"I . . . I'm not who you think I am, May."

"Constance, what are you talking about?" She laughed, but her hand tightened a bit around my arm. As if I had no choice but to stay there and finish what I'd started.

"I didn't just leave Sanford behind," I said, my voice shaking. It shook and shook, but I went on because there was no stopping now, even if I wanted to. "I was born and raised in Gumbottom, Alabama. As a Negro. I moved to San Francisco last year to start over life as . . . as a white woman."

May's hand went slack around my arm. She stumbled backward for a moment, staring at me with unblinking eyes. "Constance, are you teasing me?"

"No, I'm not teasing. I...Everything I said is true."

I felt absolutely dizzy, as if the truth had flown from my lips and was spinning me round and round at the joy of finally being let loose.

May backed all the way up until she was standing against the wall. Her face was so pale that I pulled one of the chairs out from the table and offered her my water.

"May?" I finally said, what felt like hours later.

"Take the day, Constance."

"Pardon me?"

"Take the day for yourself. Mary Ellen and I will mind the store today."

Today? Or—

"Are you firing me, May?"

"No," she replied in a whisper.

"Well, if you're sure..."

"I'll see you tomorrow, Constance."

But she didn't look at me as she spoke, and as I took my purse and left, I didn't believe I'd see her again.

I spent the rest of the day in tears. How could I have been so stupid for the second time in my new life? How did I ever expect to make a way for myself if I kept making such foolish mistakes?

That evening, there was a knock on my bedroom door. The housemistress, Mrs. Morgan, poked her head in. "You have a visitor."

I sat up on the bed, wiping my damp eyes. Was it the police? Had they finally come to take me away? Would they put me on a train back to Alabama and instruct me never to set foot in California again?

But Mrs. Morgan seemed entirely too calm to have answered the door to angry policemen. And when she moved out of the doorway, May's face appeared. She wore the same dress as earlier, and the same worried expression. She shut the door behind her and I offered her a seat, but she shook her head, standing with her back straight.

"I suppose you've come to fire me in person," I said, standing.

"Constance." She sighed. "I... That was quite a story you told me this morning."

"I'm sorry, May. I—"

"Oh, Constance. _I'm_ so sorry." She swooped in and suddenly May was _hugging_ me.

I stood stiff in her arms at first, then I relaxed. This wasn't a perfunctory hug. I could feel the warmth behind it.

"I'm so, so sorry," she said as we pulled apart. I was relieved she had the good sense to keep her voice low.

"Why are _you_ sorry?"

"Because I didn't know sooner. Because of this country. Because of all you've had to..." She shook her head. "I'm just so sorry."

I'd always known May was different. I'd never once heard her speak negatively of anyone because of their skin color or anything else they couldn't choose. Right away, she'd told me to call her by her first name because "Mrs. Schiff was

263

her mother-in-law." But I'd never expected to find anyone this understanding. This...

"Why are you being so kind to me?" I thought of Mrs. Graham, who was more concerned about appearances than my well-being. Of Mrs. Hansen and the newsstand man, who were so open about their hatred of Negroes. Of all the white Santa Barbarans I'd overheard saying nasty things about my race when they thought I was one of them.

"Because I understand," she said, her chocolate-brown eyes brimming with tears.

"Thank you, May." Of course she'd never truly understand, but the fact that I had an ally in my corner who knew the truth about me was more than I ever could have asked for.

"No, I mean, I <u>understand</u>." The tears dripped over as May leaned in close and whispered, "I'm mulatto, Constance. My mother..."

"What? You're—"

She pressed her hand over my mouth, looking past her shoulder at the door. I liked

Mrs. Morgan much better than Mrs. Hansen, but May was right. We may have found each other, but we still had to be careful.

She dropped her hand. "Another time. Very soon. I...I imagine we have a lot to talk about. But I wanted you to know." She turned to go, wiping her eyes before she opened the door. "See you tomorrow?"

"Yes, tomorrow. Good night, May."

"Good night, Constance."

It was all I could do not to tear through the house hooting with joy. I didn't just have an ally. May had quickly become what I'd considered a friend as much as a supervisor, but now...

Now I had a sister.

Love, C

20

THE ABSTRACTION

I DON'T THINK I'VE EVER BEEN MORE EXCITED FOR A three-day weekend to get here.

School has been so annoying the past few days. Our teachers are piling on more and more homework, even before the long weekend, since there's a staff development day on Monday. Edie has been talking about planning the Halloween party and seems a little better, but the closer the weekend got, the quieter she became. And Laramie...well, we're not in a fight, but we aren't talking like we used to.

When Elliott and Dad tell me to pack a bag on Friday night, I look at them suspiciously.

"Where are we going?"

"Away for the weekend. And it's a surprise, Al."

I stare at Dad. He's never been as good at keeping secrets as Elliott.

But he just shrugs. "A surprise is a surprise. And don't bother Denise, either. She knows, and she's coming with us, and she's been sworn to secrecy."

I manage not to bug them about it the rest of the evening, but I can barely sleep, wondering where we're heading off to the next day.

We're on the road by eight on Saturday morning, and I can't believe how early I've been up two weekends in a row. Dad is driving with Denise in the front seat next to him, Elliott and me in the back. I try one more time when we stop for gas: "You won't even give me a little hint about where we're going?"

Dad's eyes meet Elliott's in the rearview mirror. "Okay, how about this? We're going to a place that's a little over two hours away."

I make a face. California is so big, that could be anywhere.

I guess I must be sleepier than I thought, because as soon as we get on the 101 freeway, heading south, I rest my head on Elliott's shoulder and zonk out immediately. I don't open my eyes until he's shaking me awake, saying, "We're here, Al."

I rub my eyes and sit up, looking around as I get out of the car. We're surrounded by green lawns, Spanish-style buildings with terra-cotta roofs, and mountains looming in the distance. We could seriously be anywhere in California.

"Where are we?" I ask, squinting against the sun.

"Your birthplace," Dad says with a grin.

"Ojai?"

"The one and only," says Elliott. "We're staying at a resort because I couldn't talk your father and Denise out of their bougieness when it comes to accommodations."

"And because we could all use a little pampering and a nice pool," Denise counters. "We're getting massages, and you and I are getting manis and pedis, Alberta."

Now I'm starting to wish we went away on surprise trips more often.

"Tomorrow we'll sleep in"—yes!—"have breakfast, and stop by the old stomping grounds to see how the property is holding up before we head home," Dad says.

I visited the commune after I was born, but I don't remember anything about it. Honestly, it sounds kind of weird and boring when they talk about it, but it is kind of neat to think about the three of them living there together all those years ago.

I've never had a massage. I was worried I wouldn't like someone I don't know touching me, but it's okay. The woman who works on me has a soft voice and gentle hands. After our massages, Dad and Elliott head to the pool while Denise and I get set up with our nail techs.

"Are you scared?" I ask Denise as a woman with a tight black bun starts in on my toes. I picked a light pink polish for my toenails and a creamy sky blue for my fingers.

"About what?" Denise's voice is dreamy. She's resting her head against the spa chair with her eyes closed, and she looks so comfortable I wonder if she might have fallen asleep for a minute.

"About, you know . . . the baby," I say, gesturing to her stomach. Even though she can't see me.

Her eyes pop open. She looks down at the arm

cradling her belly. "Oh. Well, a little bit, I guess. I've done this before, and Tim and I have a birth plan, but you never know what can happen. Childbirth is a lot more dangerous than people think, and doctors are only just starting to talk about that. But I've tried to treat myself and the baby the best I can, so I'm not really scared. Excited, mostly."

I'm used to her saying "the baby" since they decided not to find out if they're having a boy or a girl. But I wonder what they'll have. This little part of me hopes it's not a girl. I stare down at my knees, wondering where that thought came from.

"I'm excited, too," I say, mostly because I feel guilty for thinking that. Denise isn't my parent, and the baby isn't really going to be my sibling, technically. But if she has a girl, will she look like her, too?

"How have things been with Laramie?" she asks, taking a sip of her cucumber water. "Are they back to normal?"

"No, not really. They're ... well, it just seems like she's so hot and cold. Sometimes she wants to talk about things and it's like nothing was ever weird between us. But sometimes I try to talk to her about the same things, and she gets annoyed and walks away."

"Hmm," Denise says after I explain what I saw at the assembly last week. "Maybe Laramie just needs to spread her wings a bit. Try out something new. That doesn't mean she has to leave you behind, though."

I wrinkle my nose. "Sometimes I wish *I* lived on the commune."

Denise laughs, not unkindly. "I think you'd choose Ewing Beach over the commune any day. It was a beautiful experience, and one of the most special places I've ever lived, but it had its flaws."

"Really? Like what?" She, Dad, and Elliott always talk about it like it was the most perfect place on Earth.

"Well, first of all, I was one of the few women at the commune. And the men were quite outspoken and overbearing when they wanted to be. I was lucky to have Elliott and Kadeem, but even though they were my best friends, they didn't really understand what it was like to be a woman there."

"Were you friends with the other women?"

"Yes, but not close friends. We were all artists of some type, but we had such different personalities." Denise sighs. "One thing I really regret about my time there was the lack of strong female friendships."

I shrug. I used to think my friendship with Laramie was strong enough to handle anything, but lately, I don't know if that's true.

"I know things are tough right now," Denise continues. "I had one of the worst fights of my life with my best friend the summer before sixth grade. I thought we'd never recover."

"What were you fighting about?"

Denise laughs. "I have no idea, but that was before cell phones, so there was a lot of secret three-way calling and hanging up and my mama telling me 'you little girls better quit playing on my phone!'"

I stare at her. "Three-way calling?"

"It's like a conference call, except you had to..." She stops, shaking her head. "It's not important. I'm a dinosaur. What I'm trying to say is that these feelings and these...hard times won't last forever. After what you've told me, I'm pretty certain this has everything to do with something Laramie is going through and nothing to do with you."

"It just seems like she's too cool for me now," I say. "And she's hanging out with someone she knows is mean to me."

"It can be hard to make sense of why people do what they do. Sometimes I don't think the people doing it even understand. But my best friend and I recovered from that god-awful fight, and I'm pretty sure you and Laramie will be okay, too."

Denise sounds so sure of it, but I'm worried she's wrong. Laramie and I haven't even had a real fight, and somehow, that seems even worse.

The next morning, after we stuff ourselves at the hotel restaurant with strawberry pancakes, we pack up our things and drive to the commune.

"Have you been here since the time I came with you?" I ask when we get there.

Dad puts the car in park at the end of a long drive that wound us through dense patches of trees. "Nope. That was the last time—when you were about five. We were heading down to see Denise and stopped on the way."

"It was exactly the same," Elliott says, staring up

at the large white farmhouse in front of us. "Almost all the same people were here."

"I haven't been since I left eleven years ago." Denise follows his gaze.

A small white man with a balding patch on top of his head and wire-rimmed glasses that sit on the edge of his nose comes out of the house. "Hey there, can I help you?"

"Oh, hello." Dad smiles at him. "We were looking for Kent."

The man frowns. "Kent?"

"Yeah, he kind of runs the place?" Elliott pauses. "Or, he used to."

"I'm sorry, are you looking for one of our writers in residence?"

Dad, Elliott, and Denise all exchange looks with one another.

"Is this not the Abstraction?"

It surprises me to hear Elliott call the commune by its name. They almost never do. It's usually just "Ojai" or "the space."

"No, this is a writers' residency," the man says, pushing his glasses up on his nose. "You're not looking for the artists who used to live here?"

"That's exactly who we're looking for," Elliott says.

The man shakes his head. "They've been gone for about two years now. We bought the property from them after a bad round of fires in the area. Said they didn't want to worry about it anymore. But the place was just about empty, anyway. There couldn't have been more than four or five people living here, including the owners."

"Kent sold the place?" Denise whispers.

Dad is blinking listlessly at the farmhouse, and Elliott's mouth hangs open.

"Sorry to break the news," the man says. "Didn't seem like an easy decision for the owners."

"How could he just sell it and not even tell us? We could've said good-bye," Dad mutters.

"Happy to let you look around if you'd like," the man offers. "I can't interrupt the writers in their cabins, but you're free to walk around the main house and the property. We did some upgrades, but…"

They all look at one another again and collectively shake their heads.

"No, but thank you. We appreciate it," Elliott says.

With his hands in his pockets, the man nods and watches us get back in the car.

"I was going to bring the baby here one day," Denise says in a voice so soft I can barely hear her.

At the last turn before the house disappears from sight, I look back at the man with glasses. He's still watching us. He looks like a tiny pin in front of the big white farmhouse.

On the way home, I see a sign for Santa Barbara through my sleepy eyes. That wakes me right up.

"Can we stop in Santa Barbara?"

"Hungry again already? I guess I could eat," Dad says. "Why don't we stop for a snack?"

"Actually...there's something I wanted to see... for school." I look between the three of them, not landing on one face for too long in case they figure out I'm lying. "A place someone used to work."

"Is this for the profile you told me about?" Denise asks.

"Mm-hmm."

"I'm impressed with how seriously you're taking this," she says, and again, I feel bad about lying to her. But not bad enough to get into Constance's whole story. I'm sort of afraid that once I tell them about her, they'll figure everything out before Edie and I can. And we're so close. I want us to do this by ourselves.

I get out my phone and look up the address to Schiff's Department Store. There's no website, but there are a ton of reviews, and pages of pictures featuring the old-fashioned sign out front.

Once we exit the freeway, I read Dad the address and he plugs it into his GPS. I feel itchy with excitement and nerves as I listen to the automated voice tell him to turn left and then right and then right again. We're only a couple of miles away.

When we pull up in front of the store, I almost expect it to be haloed in a bright light, or for there to be a sign posted in the window that says WELCOME, ALBERTA: WE'VE BEEN WAITING. The mystery of Constance is starting to feel like a scavenger hunt, and what better place to find the final clue than where she spent so much time and could almost be herself?

The storefront looks different from the old-timey pictures online, but the big red oval sign is still the same. Dad, Elliott, and Denise peer out the window.

"This is the place?" says Dad.

"Yeah, can I go in?"

Elliott gets out with me while Dad and Denise circle the block to find parking. But as soon as I start to open the door, I can tell something's off. Through the big plate-glass windows, I can see that the store is almost empty. Mostly bare clothing racks have been pushed to the sides of the store, and the tables in the center are nearly as empty, with just a few sad-looking sweaters and pairs of pants folded on top.

"What's going on here?" Elliott uses his hand as a visor to block the reflection on the glass.

"This," I say, pointing. There's a sign, all right. But it's not welcoming me. It says:

GOING OUT OF BUSINESS
ALL SALES FINAL

The door is unlocked, so I push it open and we walk in.

"Hello," a red-haired woman says from her spot behind the register. She's perched on a stool, reading a book. "We're down to the last of our inventory, but if you want it, it's yours."

"You're closing?"

"Yup." She slides her finger between the pages of her book to mark her place. "After seventy-five years in business. We couldn't compete with the online world anymore."

"What a shame," Elliott says, shaking his head. "This looks like it was a nice place. I miss department stores."

The woman gives us a sad smile. "I wish *more* people missed department stores. Can I help you find anything?"

"Actually." I step forward. "I was wondering if you might know anything about people who worked here a long time ago."

"I've been here fifteen years. Try me."

"No, I mean a *really* long time ago. Like, back in the fifties."

"Oh." She slides off the stool, abandoning her book. "Well, I'm not quite *that* old, but the business has been in my family since it opened. What's the name?"

I clear my throat, suddenly embarrassed. We're

the only three people in the store, but I feel as if I'm standing in a spotlight and have one chance to get my speech right. "Well, two people, actually. Do you know someone named Constance?"

"Constance?" She frowns, and I hold my breath, hoping she'll snap her fingers and say *Of course! She was like part of the family.* But she bites her lip and shakes her head. "The name doesn't sound familiar."

"What about a woman named May?"

Her face brightens. "May? May Schiff was my great-aunt."

My mouth drops open. "Seriously?"

"Seriously." She looks at me curiously. "How do you know her?"

"I don't. I mean, it's a long story, but I sort of know someone *she* knew.... Constance. And I'm trying to find out more about her."

"Oh, well." The sad smile is back. "I'm afraid Aunt May can't help you. She passed just last year."

No. No, no, no. Not after the phone call with Rosemary McCrimmons turned up nothing. Not when I'm *this* close to finding someone who knew Constance in real life.

"I'm sorry, honey. Most of that generation is gone.

But my father worked here when he was younger, and so did his brothers. I'm sure they'd be happy to talk to you for...?"

"It's for a school project. A profile." I've said it so many times now, even I'm starting to believe it's true.

"I could give them your number if you want?" She looks at Elliott to check.

He nods and nudges me, but I shake my head. "No, it's okay, thank you."

"Are you sure, Al? This project sounds really important."

"Well, I think May is the only one who could have helped me...but okay." I figure it can't hurt. Just in case. "Thank you."

The woman takes my name and number and promises to give it to her family. As I look at her, I think about how May told Constance she was *mulatto*, which used to be a word to describe half-black, half-white people, but is offensive now. Just like the word *Negro*, which Constance used in her journals. And if May was her great-aunt, that means somewhere in her past, this woman has black relatives, too. Which is hard to believe, with her pale skin and auburn hair. I wonder if she knows about her family's history.

Dad and Denise are still circling when we walk back out. They pull over when they see us and look back as we slide in.

"Well?" Denise says.

I shake my head. "The woman I need to talk to died."

"Sorry, sweetheart," Dad says with sympathetic eyes. "Pretty disappointing day for all of us, huh?"

I don't look back at the store as we leave. I don't want a memory of how close I came to finding out the truth.

EWING BEACH

Later, once we're home and have eaten dinner and I've said good night, I sit cross-legged on my floor with Constance's journals. I have five more, and since Edie didn't care, I looked through the years in the remaining stack and picked the last ones.

I thought a few of the books might be only half-full, deserted midway through, which has happened to me each time I've tried to start a journal. But every single page of them is filled with her writing. She kept them all through the sixties. There are a lot of pages.

I flip through 1961, 1964, 1966. I stop every few pages and scan for something about her living in a new town, going back to San Francisco, or talking to her family or Sanford down South. But there's only Constance recapping her years in Santa Barbara and her friendship with May, who never gave up her secret.

She loved it there. She worked at the department store, hung out with her friends, and spent a lot of time at the beach. When I get to those parts, I think about the old *Gidget* TV show. It was probably made around the same time Constance was writing in her journals, and I wonder if she ever got on a surfboard. She talked about going on dates sometimes, but she was worried about getting too serious in case she had to tell someone her secret and they ended up breaking things off—or worse, revealing it to everyone.

But then I get to someone she called J. She said she hadn't felt that way about anyone since she was with Sanford back home. She called some people by their initials and others by their first names, but she never wrote his out. He was just J.

I stretch out my legs and lean my back against the bed. My eyes start to droop at the end of 1967, but I keep pushing on through the last one: 1968. I smile through a yawn when I read that J proposed marriage to Constance. They had a small civil ceremony at the courthouse with just his family. I figure the next entry is going to talk about having babies, because all of her friends are getting married and having babies. Even May, whose only child, they were both relieved to see, turned out lighter than his mother. But instead—

"Oh my god!" I sit up and gasp. Rub my eyes, because it's late and the ink is faint on the page. Maybe I'm not reading this right.

April 11, 1968

J and I have made one of the biggest decisions of our lives.

We are quitting our jobs, moving up the coast, and buying a house. But not just any house—a bed and breakfast! In a sweet little tourist town called Ewing Beach. The real estate agent said it's the perfect place to start a family.

I've never owned anything so big or important in my life.

M. McCrimmons never could have owned something so big or important. But I left her behind a long time ago.

And now, no one can ever force me to move
out of their house again. I will have my own
home. My home I share with J.

> *Love, C*

I reread it again and again and again, but the words never change. And I can't believe them.

Because it looks like Constance was a whole lot closer than I thought this entire time.

22

BARNEY

I'm finishing up a late breakfast with my dads and Denise on Monday morning when the doorbell rings.

I jump up right away, hoping it's Edie. I was planning to walk over later. I've been trying to get ahold of her since last night, but she's not returning my texts or answering her phone. I keep looking at the B&B, trying to see some movement from her tiny attic window, but I don't see any sign of her being home. Ms. Whitman's car isn't in the driveway.

But when I open the door, Oliver is standing on

the porch in his wet suit, surfboard propped up next to him.

"Hey, Alberta. I'm heading down to the beach. Want to come?"

What I really want to do is talk to Edie immediately, but I can never say no to surfing. Especially on a day off from school. I've barely had time to go in the ocean since surf camp ended, and just watching isn't enough. I miss it deep in my bones.

"Let me check with my dads," I say, but before I can even turn around, Elliott calls out, "Fine with us!"

Fifteen minutes later, Oliver and I are walking down to the beach in the chilly morning air. I can already tell it's been too long since I was in the water because my arm starts cramping right away from holding my board.

"Your dads seem pretty cool," Oliver says as we walk along.

"They are pretty cool. I mean, for dads," I add quickly.

"Denise was nice, too. She looks really pregnant." He seems a bit concerned.

"Yeah, I think she's going to have the baby soon."

"Is that weird for you?"

I start to answer and then stop, because it hits me that this is the first time anyone has ever asked what it feels like for me that Denise is having another baby. Edie asked what's it like with her around, but not what it's like that she's having another child. I don't know how Oliver knew I needed that question—*I* didn't even know I needed it—but it makes me feel like he's pretty cool, too.

"Kind of? I mean, I'm happy for her and Tim. But it *is* weird. The baby is technically going to be my half sister or half brother. Except not really."

Oliver shrugs. "I don't know. I don't think it has to be *so* weird. More family is better than not enough, right?"

I think of Constance, alone in California all those years ago and missing her family. "Yeah...I guess you're right."

"Did you do anything this weekend?"

I tell him about our trip to Ojai, leaving out the stop in Santa Barbara. Oliver already knows about the commune, but it doesn't bother me when he asks questions. I tell him about the farmhouse and the open land and how sad my dads and Denise were when they found it wasn't the same place they used to live.

"That sounds like a bummer."

"It was, a little bit. But we also stayed in a fancy hotel and I got a mani-pedi and a massage, so it wasn't all bad."

"So bougie," Oliver teases.

"The bougiest."

"Well, that sounds like more fun than my weekend. My dad made me spend all of Saturday and most of yesterday after church doing soccer drills so I can get ready for the season."

I frown. "But soccer doesn't start until the spring, right?"

He rolls his eyes. "Like that matters to my dad. It's not even a question to him if I'm going to make the team. He wants me to be the best so I can make varsity with the eighth graders."

"Do you *want* to play with the eighth graders?" I shudder at the thought.

But Oliver grins. "How else will I get them to respect me?"

The beach is crowded with local families, the sun is bright, and the lifeguards are on high alert since they know schools are out for the day, scanning the water with their whistles at the ready. It takes us a while to find a good spot, but once we do, we climb down the dunes, drop our boards, and do some stretches before we head out to the water.

I'm sitting with my right leg long and my forehead touching my knee, breathing in the salty air and thinking what a perfect morning this is when the shrillest voice cuts through the peaceful ocean waves.

"Look, Shauna—it's *the best surfer in all of Ewing Beach Surf Camp!*"

I don't even have to lift my head to know it's Nicolette. I don't think anyone else's voice could be drenched in that much sarcasm. I look up to find them standing over me with their arms crossed.

I think of Dad's advice to just ignore her ignorant comments. But then I think about how she invaded my perfect day, and my anger takes over.

"Don't you have something better to do than harass us?"

"Oooh, *harass.* Someone's been studying their vocab words." Nicolette smirks, then turns to Shauna, whose snide look matches her own. Why is she so proud of herself for being so mean?

"Honestly, McKee. Find a new hobby," Oliver says. I want to high-five him.

And now I can't stop what I've started, because I add, "Yeah, did you follow us here just to make fun of us or...?"

"You wish," she scoffs. Then, in an instant, her tone turns from snotty to sticky, irritatingly sweet. "Have you talked to your *bestie* lately?"

I shake my head. I haven't seen Laramie since Friday, and we haven't talked since I texted that I was going away with my family. I feel a bit of shame when I realize that since I got back from Ojai, I've been more excited to talk to Edie than Laramie. And I think, at first, that Nicolette is trying to rub it in that she's been hanging out with her more than me. But there's something off about the way she's talking and looking at me.

"Oh, really? Never mind." Her voice is so exaggerated, she sounds like one of the drama kids at school going over their lines.

Don't take the bait, don't take the bait, don't—

"Why?"

Nicolette's eyes get big like she's said too much.

She exchanges a look with Shauna, who mirrors her expression. "Oh, nothing."

It's pretty obvious she wants me to ask again, but I know Nicolette. This won't end well. And even though I'm dying to know what she's getting at, I decide it's not worth it. I can ask Laramie myself. Besides, Ewing Beach is small enough that anything important will eventually find its way to me.

"Okay." I shrug at her and stand up, turning to Oliver. "Ready to get out there?"

"Definitely. It really stinks around here all of a sudden."

"Yeah, smells kind of like a barney to me."

We grab our boards and walk down to the water, laughing the whole way. A barney is someone who's not very good at surfing, and Nicolette knows it. I look back before we paddle out, and her face is pinched into the sourest expression ever. Mission accomplished.

Turns out she didn't ruin my perfect day after all. The water is amazing: crystal clear and cool. It's always cool on the Central Coast—borderline cold—but the fall is the best time to surf here because it brings the greatest waves.

We see a good one coming up and Oliver points toward it, getting my permission to go for it. He's closest to the peak, so I wave him on and watch as he pops up and crouches, riding it smooth as butter. If he's this good at soccer, his dad might have a point about varsity.

I don't think I'm going to take off on the next one, but at the last minute I catch it with a flawless pop-up and launch into a bottom turn, maneuvering my body toward the lip. Then, as the wave starts to break, I bend my knees even lower and, gaining speed, shift my weight and try to ride along the lip of the wave. I don't last long before I go under, but I guess it's long enough because when I come back up, Oliver is cheering for me instead of waiting for the next wave to roll in.

"Nice floater!" he yells, water dripping from his raised victory fists.

I smile as I take a minute to catch my breath. Competing may be what I really want to do, but I guess my dads weren't totally wrong. Just having fun with surfing is still...fun.

BRAVE CHOICES

LARAMIE IS ABSENT ON TUESDAY. EVEN THOUGH I'M kind of glad we don't have to sit across from each other at the lunch table being awkward, I send her a text to check in, remembering how Nicolette asked about her yesterday at the beach. She says she's fine, just home with a sick stomach.

Edie is in a slightly better mood. When I saw her in math class, she apologized for not getting back to me until late yesterday. Her mom took her on a last-minute trip to Santa Cruz over the long weekend. I saw their car pull into the driveway after dark, when

I was already getting ready for bed. When she texted back, I told her I had something to tell her today.

She tells the guys about the Halloween party and says they're all invited. She doesn't even say anything to Jamie when he mumbles that it must be her favorite holiday. She just arches her eyebrow so fiercely that he doesn't utter another word.

I'm practically bursting by the time school is over. The 1968 journal is buried at the bottom of my backpack, but I can feel it burning hot as Edie and I walk home.

"Want to stop by Coleman Creamery?" I ask as we get to the main drag.

"I thought you had something to tell me." She's looking down at her phone, but the screen is black and she's not actually using it. Just staring, like she's willing it to do something.

"I do, but I can tell you over ice cream. Leif's treat." I'm a little worried I won't be able to make it the few blocks home. Every time I think about the journal, I feel itchy trying to keep the news in.

"Okay, but my dad is supposed to call sometime before dinner, so I might have to talk to him."

A few of the restaurants in town shut down for

the year once the summer is over, but Coleman Creamery is open off-season. Usually only a few hours a day, but always after school. And it's always packed with kids doing homework, shouting over one another, and making Leif's job difficult.

He's working today and looks relieved to see us when we walk in. "Finally, someone I can talk to. I just had to break up an ice-cream fight over there," he says, pointing to a table of sixth graders. "How's it going?"

"It's going good," I say.

Edie smiles at him but doesn't say anything.

"Butter pecan, Alberta?" Leif asks, wielding the scooper in his plastic-gloved hand.

I start to say yes, but then I stop. I think about Constance and all the brave choices she made in her life. She took chances, even when she knew how scary it could be. I've always gotten butter pecan because I know I like it and won't be disappointed... but it's just ice cream. If I hate whatever I try, I can get butter pecan the next time.

"Actually... I want to try something new. You can choose."

"You got it, boss." He paces behind the case with his eyes narrowed as he studies the tubs of ice cream.

He stops, pointing his scoop to the front row. "There it is. Honey rhubarb. You want a taste?"

"No...I trust you." I watch him dig out a heaping scoopful. "Hey, is Laramie okay? She said she had a stomachache."

Leif rolls his eyes. "I guess. She barely talks to me since school started. She about bit my head off when I asked her if she had any plans on Saturday. I just wanted to know if she needed a ride anywhere."

"Yeah...she's been like that with me, too." And, to be honest, I'm relieved that it's not just me.

He sighs, handing me the cup of ice cream. "Middle school girls, man." Then he pauses. "High school girls, too. You're all tough to figure out."

"Like you guys are so much better," Edie says, talking for the first time since we walked in. Her eyes flit over the ice-cream case. "Can I get a scoop of rocky road in a cone?"

I slide a bite of ice cream on my tongue and let it melt. I close my eyes. I haven't had anything but butter pecan in years. And this is amazing. It's tart and sweet and light at the same time. I eat half my cup before Leif has even scooped up Edie's rocky road.

When he walks out to the floor to wipe down

tables, I pull out the journal, open it to the entry I read last night, and push it in front of Edie.

But she's not paying attention. She's still looking at her phone, even though it hasn't lit up once since we left school.

"He'll call," I say in my best encouraging voice. "And you're going to see him again. I'm sure he feels really bad that he—"

"That's easy for you to say, Alberta! You have *so many* people here who..." She stops, takes a shaky breath, and goes on. "You have *two* dads, and now you have your bio mom, and—you don't get it. My dad is my favorite person on the planet and everyone's acting like it's okay that I'll only get to see him a few times a year now."

"I'm sorry," I say. And I really mean it. She's right. I don't know what it's like to have divorced parents. Or a dad I only get to talk to over the phone.

"Well, if you're sorry, then stop telling me it's going to be okay," Edie snaps. "I'm tired of hearing that, especially from someone who has no idea what it's like. It's not going to be okay until I get to see my dad."

I shrink into myself like she slapped me. Edie has

been quiet lately. Cranky, for sure. But she's the one who kept telling me everything was fine with her dad. And she's never talked to me like that. Her voice seeps into me like venom. I drop my spoon; the ice cream is sour on my tongue.

Denise said Laramie's moodiness probably has nothing to do with me, and I know Edie's doesn't, either. But *I'm* tired of people snapping at me when I'm just trying to be a good friend to them.

I hop down from the stool, zip up my backpack, and push my shoulders through the straps.

"Where are you going?"

"Home. It's the only place nobody's ever mad at me."

"Alberta—"

"You should read that journal." I stab my finger at the book in front of her. The book she never even bothered to look at, after all the time we've spent trying to figure this out. "*That's* what I wanted to tell you. I think Constance used to own the B&B. Mrs. Harris was passing for white."

Edie's eyes widen. "Alberta, wait—"

But I stalk away from her, straight for the door. The mooing cow is the last sound I hear.

ACCIDENT

I FEEL A STRANGE ENERGY IN THE AIR AS SOON AS I walk into school Wednesday morning.

I can tell right away that it's not about me, because the students standing around barely give me a second glance. But I sense people are talking about *something*. There's a buzz in the atrium, and people keep giggling behind their hands. And the worst part is I can't even ask Edie if I'm imagining it.

Last night after dinner, I found a text from her apologizing. She asked if I wanted to talk about Constance. I *did* want to talk about Constance, but I was still too upset with her. Dad and Denise kept asking me if something was wrong, and I just said I had a lot of homework I wasn't looking forward to. Which wasn't totally false.

But when I sat down to do my reading, all I could think about was how it seems like I never know the right thing to say to my friends anymore. Somehow, Edie snapping at me hurt more than when Laramie did. We don't get in a lot of fights or anything, but I've known Laramie longer. And for Edie to not be interested in the journals...well, that hurt, too. Constance has taken up so much of our time over the last few weeks, and Edie ruined the big reveal. Plus, it was our *thing*. The one thing we both cared about enough to work on like it was an assignment. The one thing we shared that no one else from school would understand the way we do.

I finally texted back that maybe we could talk about the journals soon. Even though I was dying to know what she thought, and if Mrs. Harris had left behind anything else, and if Ms. Whitman knew anything about the situation. When Edie texted back that she had a dentist appointment the next morning and would see me at lunch, my shoulders sagged in relief.

I say hi to a few people on the way to my locker,

but nobody tells me what's going on. As I'm opening my locker door, I see Nicolette and Gavin walking this way. She has her arm looped through his and he's smirking as they saunter through the hallway to the eighth-grade wing, looking like they own the school. She catches my eye and gives me a nasty look. I roll my eyes and stare right back until she looks away.

I stop in the bathroom before homeroom, even though first bell is in four minutes. But I don't want to go all the way to Mr. Simons's room, get the bathroom pass, and come back, so I chance it. I can always run.

I'm washing my hands when I hear something behind me. I thought I was the only one in here, and when I look under the stalls, I don't see any feet. I shut off the faucet, soapy water dripping from my fingers. The room is silent. But when I turn on the water, I swear I hear it again.

The faucet squeaks off. "Hello?"

Still nothing.

I dry my hands with a scratchy paper towel and go down the short line of stalls. The door to the last one is partially shut, and when I push it open, Laramie's teary brown eyes are staring back at me.

"What are you doing in here?"

She's squatting over the closed lid of the toilet, her back against the stall wall and her feet planted on the seat. Her face is a splotchy pink and her curls are a mess, like she's been running her hand through them over and over again.

"I need to go home," she whispers.

"Is it your stomach? Do you want to go to the nurse?"

Her tears well over, splashing down her cheeks. "It's not my *stomach*, Alberta. It's...Nicolette."

I stare at her. "What do you mean?"

"Are you sure we're alone?" she chokes out between thick sobs.

I drop my backpack on the floor, check each stall again, and then come back to hers. "It's just us. What's wrong, Laramie?"

She sniffles loudly. "Nicolette...she said..." Laramie tries to tell me, but her words keep coming out in chokes and hiccups. The bell rings. She flinches and looks at me. "You should go so you don't get in trouble."

I shrug. "It's just homeroom. Simons won't get mad if I tell him I was helping someone. Laramie... what did she say?"

"I...I spent the night at her house when you were gone last weekend. On Saturday. And I told her that Gavin...that Gavin tried to kiss me the other day. After school."

My mouth drops open. "He *did*?"

Laramie's had her first kiss, too?

"He tried, but...I pushed him away. And I told Nicolette because I thought that's what a friend should do." She swallows. "You guys were right. Nicolette has a crush on him. But she told me first, so it felt like I couldn't like him, too."

"What did she say?"

"She pretended like everything was fine when I told her. Like she wasn't mad at me. But then, the next day...she started telling people I had an accident all over her bed and she has to get a new mattress."

"She told people you *wet the bed*?"

"No." Laramie shakes her head and squeezes her eyes shut. Her voice is barely audible when she says, "My period."

My stomach seizes. *That's* what people were laughing about this morning? And I guess that's why no one bothered to tell me what was going on. "Is it true?"

"No! She's just being awful because of the Gavin

stuff. After I told her about the kiss, I said I'd had a crush on him, but I wasn't going to do anything since she liked him first. The rumor started with just a few of her friends, then it spread. And now it's all over the school today." She frowns through her tears. "I saw *sixth graders* giving me weird looks this morning."

I put my hand on her arm. "Why didn't you tell me about any of this? About the kiss and—"

"Because you hated Nicolette and Gavin. And you've been, like, attached at the hip with Edie since she moved here."

"We haven't been attached at the hip."

"You walk to and from school together *every day*. You go over to the B&B all the time, or she's at your house. You were so excited when she moved here, and I felt…I don't know. When Nicolette started being nice to me, I figured you wouldn't even notice. It felt like you'd been waiting your whole life for Edie to move in across the street."

I put my hand on her arm. "I'm sorry, Laramie. I…" I want to explain how good it feels to finally have someone here who understands the parts of me she'll never know. I want to tell her about the journals and how they connect Edie and me with a part of being black that *we're* still trying to understand. But now is not the time.

"I guess you were right about Nicolette." She lets out a shuddery breath.

I'm not thinking about how I was right, though. All I can think about is how sad and hurt my best friend looks right now.

I put my arms around her so her sobs muffle into my shirt instead of echoing through the cold, empty bathroom.

Laramie eventually stopped crying long enough to call her mom and ask to go home. I walked her to the office before I went to homeroom, and when the secretary saw the shape Laramie was in, she was nice enough to write me a late pass.

The guys are on their best behavior at lunch. They obviously know what people are saying about Laramie, but they don't mention it. Edie arrives from her dentist appointment with a bag of fresh In-N-Out, including fries for the whole table.

"Well?" Jamie says after Edie takes a bite of her burger.

Around us, everyone is staring enviously at Edie. The cafeteria is serving Philly cheesesteaks today; the guys couldn't shut up about how good they were earlier, but now they're picking at their lunches. They're savoring the fries like they've never had them before in their life. Even Fletcher is eating them one by one, rationing so they can last through the end of lunch.

"Fine, it's a good burger," she says, rolling her eyes. She doesn't come up for air again until she's half-done.

Edie walks up to my locker after school just as I finish looking at my phone. Laramie hasn't responded to my texts. I hope she's okay.

"Hey," Edie says.

"Oh, hey." I was relieved we didn't have to walk to school together this morning, but I forgot about getting home. I slip my phone into my pocket.

"I was thinking maybe we could talk about Constance? You're totally right. She *has* to be Mrs. Harris."

"Um, yeah," I say, stuffing my history textbook into my bag. "But can we get together another time? I need to go check on Laramie."

Edie is quiet for a moment. "Oh. Is she okay?"

"I think so, but I want to check, just to make sure."

"Should I come with you?"

I pause. "I don't know, Edie. I think she might not want a lot of people around."

"Oh, okay. Right." She nods, gripping the strap of her bag. "Well, I guess I'll see you later."

"Yeah, see you later."

I wish I felt good about being so cool to Edie. I don't want to be mean to her, but my feelings are still hurt by the way she snapped at me and how she brushed off my discovery about Constance after all the work we've done.

But as I watch her walk away, hair hanging like a sheet over her face, I wonder if she ever heard from her dad.

And I don't feel good about watching her walk away, but I don't stop her, either.

SLEEPOVER

When I get home from Laramie's, the house is completely empty. No Dad, no Denise, and no Elliott, even though he should be returning home from work right about now.

I go to the kitchen to look for a note, but there's nothing. Just as I pull my phone from my bag to call Dad, the screen lights up. He's calling.

"Alberta, are you home?"

"I just got back from Laramie's. Where are you?"

"Up in SLO," he says, and his voice sounds strange, but I can't figure out why. Too distant? Nervous? It's ... something.

"With Elliott?"

"No, but he's on his way. To the hospital. I'm with Denise—she went into labor right before you got out of school! She didn't want to risk driving down to L.A. to have the baby, so her doula is making the trip to meet us up here. Tim is still in Vancouver, but he's trying to get on the next flight down."

Through all his babble, only one thing sticks out: "Denise is going to have her baby?"

"Denise is going to have her baby," he confirms, and I think I know now what's in his voice. He sounds a little weepy, like he might cry at any second. The same way he sounds when we watch nature documentaries about animals in the wild with their babies.

"Is someone coming down to get me?" I wonder if we'll spend the night. Should I pack a bag? Will I get to stay home from school tomorrow? SLO is only twenty minutes away, but it's not every day that someone we know has a baby. When *my* birth mother has a baby.

"That's why I'm calling," Dad says, and I can tell by the way his tone shifts into apologetic that I won't be spending the night in San Luis Obispo. "Since Elliott is already up here, it makes more sense for him not to come down right now, or for either of us to deal with rush-hour traffic. Denise wants him in the room."

"Can't I take a car or something?"

"Alberta Freeman-Price, I am not letting you 'take a car' by yourself up here. *You're* still *my* baby."

I huff. "So when do I get to come up?"

"I'm not sure yet. But Elliott or I will come down and pick you up as soon as we can, okay? The baby isn't even here yet. And I've called Calliope, who is more than happy to have you stay over at the B&B tonight and see you off to school in the morning. Sound good?"

It doesn't sound good at all, really. I think of Edie walking away after school today. Now I have to spend the night with her?

"Dad, please. I promise I won't be any trouble—"

"Sweetheart, I need you to be a little more agreeable," Dad says in his voice that means he's trying his best to sound patient. "This makes the most sense, and I promise you'll be up here in no time. Be good for the Whitmans. We'll call you as soon as there's more news."

Dad hangs up and I stand with my phone in my

hand, looking around my empty kitchen. I can't believe my entire family is only twenty minutes away and I have to stay here, wondering when I get to be with them. Wondering how Edie feels about me spending the night.

I jump as the doorbell rings. When I open the front door, Edie is standing behind it, pink bakery box in hand.

"I don't know how to bake anything, but I stopped and got these cookies for you." She holds the box out in front of her. "I didn't know what kind you like, so I got one of everything. Do you even like cookies?"

"I love cookies," I say, staring down at the box.

I can't believe she went to the bakery to get these for me when I blew her off this afternoon.

Edie is quiet for a moment. Then she says, "I didn't mean to be rude to you at the creamery, and... it wasn't cool. I'm sorry."

I take the cookies from her and tuck the box under my arm, shifting my weight from foot to foot. "Thanks. And... it's okay. I'm sorry, too. About your dad. I was just so excited about the Constance stuff, but I know how much you miss him."

She sighs. "It's not just that I miss him anymore. I

guess... I'm wondering if he is who I thought he was, you know? He doesn't visit when he says he's going to. And now he doesn't call when he says he's going to. And... I'm pretty sure he cheated on my mom."

My eyes widen. "That's why they got divorced?"

"Maybe? I don't know. I didn't believe it could be true at first. Craig still doesn't. He's on our dad's side and keeps blaming this on my mom for not being... *enough*, whatever that means. And I keep wondering if it's my fault."

"What? Why would it be your fault?"

"My dad didn't like it when I started dressing this way... back in fifth grade. And I started wearing black lipstick last year. I told him that it was the most me I've ever been, but he said people think goth girls are weird, and he didn't want them to treat me bad because of it."

I can't believe her father would say something like that. My dads don't love everything I want to do or wear, but I don't think they'd say people will think I'm *weird*. And I *do* feel bad for listening to what Nicolette told Laramie, and ever believing—even for a second—that Edie could be a poser, trying to fool us into thinking she's someone she's not. But then, even if she had reinvented her look just before she moved, it wouldn't have made me like her any less. Edie is Edie, no matter what she looks like.

"I guess I just...I thought my dad was, like, perfect all this time. But now...I don't know."

"That really sucks, Edie."

"Yeah, it does."

"And I don't think you're weird. I think you're probably the coolest person who's ever lived in Ewing Beach."

Her light skin blushes. "You don't have to say that."

"I'm not just saying that! I've lived here practically my whole life. It's totally true."

She blinks at me with eyes that look a bit scared. "Are we cool, Alberta? I don't think I can stand to lose my only friend in Ewing Beach right now."

"Of course we're cool," I say softly. "And I'm not your only friend."

"You're my only *real* friend." Her eyes drift down to the bakery box. "Mom says you're spending the night. Want to eat a bunch of cookies and spoil our dinner before we go back?"

I pop open the box. "Only if you let me have the oatmeal raisin."

She smiles a big, genuine smile that travels all the way down from her eyes to her mouth. "Deal."

When we get to the bed and breakfast with my overnight bag and half a box of cookies, Ms. Whitman is fussing about what we'll do for dinner, excited that I'll be spending the night with them. "You'll be our first guest in the B&B," she says proudly. "This can be our soft opening."

Edie sighs. "Mom."

But her mother's cheerfulness is so contagious it makes me feel better that I'm staying here if I can't be at the hospital. Dad didn't suggest I go to Laramie's, and even though I'm still worried about her, I didn't ask to.

We help Ms. Whitman with dinner. She found a recipe for cauliflower Bolognese sauce that she's been wanting to try. Edie appears less than thrilled, but her mother ignores the look on her face as she puts us to work making garlic butter for the bread and chopping vegetables for the salad.

"I think we should tell her," Edie whispers when her mom is across the kitchen, busy with the food processor.

I look up from the cucumber on my cutting board. "About Constance?"

"Yeah, she can help us figure out what to do."

Like if we should tell Mrs. Palmer about the journals. And how.

I've never had the kind of Bolognese with meat sauce, but I like this one. Even with my stomach full of cookies. And Edie looks pleasantly surprised as she takes a second bite.

"This is really good, Mom," she says. "I can't even tell there's cauliflower in here."

Ms. Whitman beams.

As Edie spoons more sauce into her bowl, she glances at me, then looks at her mother. "Mom, do you know anything about Mrs. Harris?"

"Mrs. Harris..." her mother says, looking toward the ceiling as if she's trying to remember who that is.

"The woman who owned the B&B before us."

"Oh, of course." Ms. Whitman reaches for a piece of garlic bread. "Well, not really. I know that she passed away here, and she lived a long life, and she was sentimental."

"What do you mean?" I ask, twirling spaghetti onto my fork.

"Her family didn't take a lot of her things. It wasn't junk, but mementos. Things that clearly meant a lot to her, from years ago."

"Well." Edie pauses and looks at me again before she goes on. "I think we found one of those mementos. Or, a few of them."

"Journals," I say. "A whole box of them, up in the attic."

Edie sets down her fork. "They don't have her name in them, but we think she was using a fake name."

"We think she was passing. For white," I add when I see the confused look on Ms. Whitman's face.

She slowly chews the rest of her garlic bread, looking back and forth between the two of us. "Girls, slow down and start over. You think Mrs. Harris was pretending to be someone else?"

We start from the beginning, and while I'm telling her about what was in the journals, Edie runs upstairs. When she comes back, she has a few cradled in her arms. Including the last one, where Constance mentions Ewing Beach.

Ms. Whitman wipes her mouth, pushes her plate aside, and opens one of the books. Her eyes scan over a few entries in a row. She looks up at us. "How many of these did you read?"

"A *lot*. From, like, 1955 to this last one," Edie says, opening the 1968 journal.

Ms. Whitman is quiet, smoothing her palms over the fragile, yellowed pages of the books. When she looks up at us, her eyes are shining. "Oh, girls. You read all of these?"

Edie and I exchange a look.

"Sorry," Edie says. "I know they're personal and I'm not supposed to read people's personal things. But they were just up there...and they're so old, we figured whoever they belonged to isn't still alive, anyway."

"No, no, I'm not mad." Ms. Whitman narrows her eyes, thinking. "I'm just trying to figure out how we could confirm it's her." Then she says, "Oh, of course!" again, and hops out of her seat.

"Mom?" Edie says, but Ms. Whitman is already heading down the hallway, mumbling to herself about some kind of paperwork.

She returns empty-handed. "We need the title to the B&B."

Edie and I just stare at her, puzzled.

"It's a record of everyone who ever owned the house and a bunch of other information that most people don't read unless they have a reason to," she says. "Mrs. Harris left the house to her kids, so the sale went through them. I don't have her name on any of my paperwork."

"Well, where can we find it? This title?" Edie tears nervously at her garlic bread.

"The county clerk's office, usually," her mother says. "But I'm thinking...since you've been working with Mrs. Palmer, maybe we should go up there and ask her ourselves."

Edie raises her eyebrow. "You mean, just...*ask* her? If her mom was passing for white?"

"We'll do it a bit more eloquently than that," Ms. Whitman says. "We can tell her we found something that we think was her mother's and would like to return. She might end up telling us herself...if she knew."

"Can we go tonight?"

Her mother looks at the clock in the dining room. "I think it's too late for tonight. Everything closes early here. But we can go tomorrow, for sure."

"You won't go without me, will you?" I ask. I want to see Denise and her baby as soon as I can, but I don't want to miss out on talking to Mrs. Palmer. Or watching Edie's mom talk to Mrs. Palmer, I guess.

"I promise we won't do it without you, Alberta," Ms. Whitman assures me.

"How could we?" Edie adds. "You're the one who figured it out."

Dad checks in before I go to bed to say the baby still hasn't come, but Tim is on a flight down to SLO. I'm disappointed. I really wanted the baby to be born by now so I could maybe go up there tonight. Now I'll have to suffer through school all day tomorrow, wondering when it's going to happen. How am I supposed to sleep with all of this going on?

Ms. Whitman says I can have my pick of rooms. They're nice rooms. A few of them are ready for guests with crisp sheets and plumped pillows on the beds, books on the nightstands, and vases on the bureaus, waiting for fresh flowers. But they all seem too big. Too far away from Edie and Ms. Whitman. So, creepy as Edie's bedroom is, I still think I'd rather sleep up there with her poster of that cranky guy and the bird than by myself.

We blow up an air mattress and Edie's mother brings up sheets and extra pillows. "You're sure you'll be okay up here, Alberta? The beds really are comfortable."

"I'll be okay. Thank you, Ms. Whitman."

"Well, if you change your mind, the offer stands. Good night, girls." She kisses Edie on the forehead and squeezes my arm before she goes back downstairs.

I figure Edie and I will stay up talking for a while, the way Laramie and I always do during sleepovers. And it always takes me longer to fall asleep in a strange place. But we both must be so exhausted by everything that's happened, because we fall fast asleep.

I wake to my phone buzzing on the pillow beside me.

I look around, confused about where I am. The room and night sky are still dark. But then I hear Edie snoring lightly in her bed and I remember.

I look at the lit-up screen. It's Elliott.

"Hey, Al," he says when I pick up. His voice is

low, but he sounds happy. A little emotional, even. "The baby's here."

I sit up on the air mattress. "Since when?"

"Just about a half hour ago—the official time was 2:02 a.m. It's a boy."

I grin. "What's his name?"

"Caleb Elliott Kaplan." He sounds proud.

"Hey, that's pretty cool," I whisper, settling back on the mattress.

"Yeah, it's pretty cool. You doing okay? Sorry the baby didn't come earlier. We all wanted you here."

"I'm fine. Can I come up tomorrow?"

That means we have to hold off another day on talking to Mrs. Palmer, but I don't think I can wait to see Denise and the baby.

"You sure can. Dad will pick you up at school."

"Are you coming home tonight?"

"Eventually. I think we're all too excited to do much of anything right now besides stare at this beautiful baby."

"Thanks for calling."

"Good night, Al. Love you."

"Love you, too," I say, closing my eyes.

CALEB

DAD IS SO GIDDY ON THE WAY TO THE HOSPITAL THE next afternoon, he barely stops talking. I don't think he got very much sleep last night. As happy as he is, there are bags under his eyes. And he keeps sipping from a giant travel mug of coffee every few minutes.

"I can't believe they gave the baby Elliott's name," I say, thinking back to his late phone call. I'm not feeling so full of energy myself. I kept waking up the rest of the night, excited about something and forgetting why. Over and over again. By the time Edie's alarm went off, I was exhausted.

"He's pretty touched," Dad says with a small

smile. He must feel me staring at him, because he finally looks over. "What?"

"Nothing."

"Alberta?"

"It's just... are you sad that she didn't name the baby after you?" I'm scared that he'll tell me it's too rude of a question, but I want to know.

"It's sweet of you to think of me, but no, I'm not," he says. "Denise and Elliott knew each other before I ever came into the picture. They just have a certain... *something*, you know? I love them both very much, but I'd never try to pretend that we all share the same friendship. Besides, Denise gave me the greatest gift of all when she gave me you."

"Dad," I say, looking down at my lap. But it makes me smile.

I get nervous when we turn into the hospital parking lot. I don't know why. I don't come to hospitals very often. Or ever, really.

"Ready?" Dad says, already out of the car. I'm still looking at the building.

Inside, there are people crowding the hallways and waiting rooms, and it smells too clean, as if everything has been dipped in bleach. I walk close to Dad, like if I hang back too far I'll get trapped in here forever.

I don't know what to expect when we get to Denise's room. Will she be hooked up to machines or woozy from medicine?

Dad knocks on the door and I hear Tim's voice telling us to come in. When we walk through the doorway, everything looks totally normal. Denise and Tim are in the room, looking just like Denise and Tim. Only their faces are just so *happy*. Like they haven't stopped smiling for the past twelve hours. They look like Elliott sounded last night.

Denise's face lights up even more when she sees us. "Alberta, we were just talking about you," she says from the bed, where she's propped up against a pile of pillows. "I'm so glad you're here."

"Me too." I stand in place until Dad gently presses my back, pushing me toward the bed.

"We were telling Caleb about how you're the best kid we know, so he has a lot to live up to," Tim says.

That's such a nice thing to say, I don't know how to respond. I look at the baby. He's a bundle in Denise's arms, wrapped in soft blankets. A tiny cap is perched on his head.

Denise plants a soft kiss on his forehead. "Are you ready to meet Alberta?" she whispers.

She turns him toward me when I reach the bed. When I realize she's holding him out, I shake my head and take a step back.

"You don't want to hold him?"

"I'm…I don't want to drop him." Or breathe on him wrong. Or hold him too tightly. He's so new, it feels like there are a billion ways to break him.

"You won't drop him. Babies are a lot stronger than people think." But when I just stand there staring at her with my skeptical face, she smiles and says, "Go sit over there in the chair and Tim will bring him to you."

I'm still feeling shaky when Tim places the swaddled baby in my arms. But I sit back, take a deep breath, and try to remember what Denise said. I stare down at Caleb. Newborn babies look funny. They're all squishy, and they're never awake. And when their eyes are open, they always look so confused and sleepy.

His eyes are closed now. Everything about him is so teeny. His little nose and chin and ears. The cap on his head is knit into the features of a baby fox.

He smells good, too—clean and sweet, like milk. He opens his mouth and yawns, showing his little gums. My heart feels like it is melting.

"He's so sweet," I say. "So little."

"He's perfect," Dad says.

Caleb's skin is a tawny color now, the perfect blend of Denise's and Tim's skin tones. I was super light when I was born. I wonder if his color will darken like mine did. He'll be beautiful no matter what.

Denise clears her throat. "Alberta, Tim and I want to ask you something."

"And we think now is the perfect time," Tim adds.

I finally look up from the baby. I think I could stare at him for hours.

"We were wondering," Denise says slowly, "if you would do us the honor of being Caleb's godmother."

I look back and forth between the two of them. "His godmother?" I feel like someone has funneled me into an alternate reality. I never expected someone to ask me this.

"We'd love if you would consider it."

"What does it mean? Being a godparent?" I don't think I have a godmother or a godfather. Do I? I look at Dad.

"Well, Denise and I aren't religious, so it's more in a spiritual sense," Tim explains.

"Your father and Elliott have always been like family," she says. "And you are, too. You've grown into such a wonderful young lady that we're just so proud to know, Alberta. We'd really love you to have a relationship with Caleb as he grows up."

"He'll be lucky to know you, too," Tim says.

They are still smiling, but they look nervous. Do they think I'll say no? Denise and Tim are reason enough to say yes, but when I look down at Caleb's squishy little face, I can't think of anyone else's godmother I'd rather be.

"Yes," I say. "Yes, please. I want to be his godmother."

Denise's eyes well up. "We're so glad."

Dad comes over to give me a hug, rubbing the back of his finger over one of Caleb's chubby cheeks. Tim snaps a picture of us, and Denise is brushing tears from her face as she watches.

The only person missing is Elliott, who's at work. But then I look down at Caleb Elliott in my arms.

He's here in name.

FAMILY

EDIE CLUTCHES THE METAL BOX TIGHTLY IN THE front seat of Ms. Whitman's car.

I stare at it. All the journals are in there. We stacked them in order from top to bottom. It's weird to think we're letting go of them now, after spending so much time with them over the past few weeks. What if Mrs. Palmer doesn't want them? What if it's not her mother and we've made a huge mistake?

As we bump along Ewing Street, toward the library, I want to go back. I didn't tell my dads about this, and I hope Mrs. Palmer doesn't get angry with us and tell them before I can. I haven't kept a lot of secrets from them—at least nothing this big.

It's Friday afternoon, and I'm happy to see the library is mostly empty. I let Ms. Whitman and Edie go ahead of me, but Mrs. Palmer greets me first with a big smile. Then she says hi to Edie, and turns to Ms. Whitman.

"Calliope, right?"

"Great memory," Edie's mother says. "It's nice to see you again."

"Same. We really should be running into each other more in such a small town." Her eyes slide curiously over the box in Edie's arms. "Can I help you all with anything today?"

Edie looks at Ms. Whitman, who nods encouragingly. She steps up to the desk and says, "We have something that we think belongs to you."

"We think it belonged to your mother," I add, standing next to her.

Mrs. Palmer frowns, but she moves aside a stack of books to make room for the box. Edie sets it down and slowly slides it toward her. "We found these in the attic of the B&B." Her voice is thin. Nervous.

Mrs. Palmer looks to Ms. Whitman before she carefully opens the box. Her eyebrows push together.

"They're journals," I explain.

"And we think…" Edie begins, but she can't finish.

"The girls read the journals," her mother says, taking the spot on the other side of Edie. "They were in a corner of Edie's bedroom in this box. And the girls think they belonged to your mother."

"Was your mom's name Constance?" Edie blurts, her courage returning.

Mrs. Palmer looks confused as she picks up one of the books. "Constance?" She flips it open and begins reading. Her eyes widen. "This is Mama's handwriting."

Edie stares at me, her eyes even bigger than Mrs. Palmer's.

I pull the two old photographs from my notebook, where I've been keeping them safe, and place them on top of the books. Constance's picture is on top.

Mrs. Palmer breathes in and out slowly. "And this is Mama."

"The girls think—" Ms. Whitman begins, but then someone comes in who needs help.

Mrs. Palmer barely hides her impatience as she plucks a book off the holds shelf. The whole time she helps the person, I notice her hands are trembling. As soon as the patron walks out the door again, she sighs heavily. She looks in the box. "This must be years' worth."

"About thirteen, I think," I say.

"And you read them all? Did you...?" Mrs. Palmer looks like she's doing calculations in her head. She flips open the journal on top to the page with Constance's name and the year. She runs her fingers over the fragile paper. "I don't know much about my mother's life. She never talked about anything before marrying our father...not until she was nearing the end."

"Was her middle name Constance?" Edie tries again.

"I don't know," Mrs. Palmer says, her eyes flitting back and forth from the journals to the pictures. "She always said she had no middle name. But I saw her driver's license one time. And the middle initial was a *C*. Matilda C. Harris. When I asked her about it, she told me to stop being nosy and changed the subject."

"Her middle name started with a *C*?" I say. Even though I thought we were right, I still can't believe things are adding up.

"So if you read them, you must know." Mrs. Palmer tilts her head to the side.

Edie and I exchange another look.

"That my mother was passing as a white woman," she says softly. "For almost her entire life."

Edie lets out a breath big enough for both of us. I'm holding mine.

"You knew," Ms. Whitman says.

"I always suspected there was something she wasn't telling us." Mrs. Palmer pauses. "I asked why our hair was so curly. And about our skin. She said we had Italian ancestry, and maybe some Jewish on our father's side. We don't look totally European, but we don't exactly look black, either. She told us the truth when our father died. She didn't want there to be any chance of him knowing."

"But they loved each other," Edie says. "Would he have cared?"

"My father was a good man, and he was good to my mother. But I...I don't know if she kept it from him because she was afraid he'd leave her or because the secret was so much a part of her." Mrs. Palmer runs her index finger along the edge of the metal box. "I think she felt like she needed to come clean before she died. She wanted us to know at least a little bit about where we came from."

"Have you found any of her family? I mean, your family?" I ask.

Mrs. Palmer shakes her head. "My grandparents are long gone by now. And Mama said her brother was, too. My brother and sister were glad to know, but they have no interest in visiting the past. I didn't look too hard after Mama told us, but now...Well, it seems like these journals are a sign to start looking again."

"Family should know family," Ms. Whitman says quietly.

Mrs. Palmer nods. "Yes, they should."

"Did she tell you why she left? And started passing?" Edie asks.

"She was pretty vague about that, too. But in those times...it could have been anything. I know that there was some violence that involved someone close to her."

Edie and I glance at each other. Sanford?

Just then, Jordan the tortie pads across the counter, curls herself into a cat loaf right in front of Mrs. Palmer, and starts purring up a storm. As if she knew Mrs. Palmer needed her.

"I know she left a man she loved, but she felt like it was the only choice for a good life. I'll never forget—" Mrs. Palmer's voice breaks and she scratches under Jordan's chin. She breathes in and out before she goes on. "I'll never forget, when Mama told us—she said that before she left, she promised her mother she'd send money once she got settled. And my grand-mother told her that she didn't want the money of a black woman pretending to be white. That it was dirty, dishonest money. She told my mother that if she was going to leave on those terms, she didn't want to see or hear from her again."

"Wow," Ms. Whitman breathes.

"I know." Mrs. Palmer lets out a heavy sigh. "The thing is, this wasn't that long ago, that people felt like this was their only option. It makes me sick to think she believed she had to live another life to get the equality she deserved."

"How will you find your family?" I ask. "She

didn't give a lot of details about her life before California."

"Something tells me you've already done some research on her yourselves." She smiles as she looks between Edie and me. "The microfilm?"

We nod, embarrassed. Busted.

"I'll find a way," she says. "I'm a librarian, after all. Who's better at finding information than us?"

"Oh!" Edie says suddenly. "We did find someone. With the last name McCrimmons. Maybe you can talk to her. She said Juanita, from the photo, was a distant cousin, so that means you'd be related, too, right?"

"I think that's exactly what that means," Mrs. Palmer says with a smile as I rip the page with Rosemary McCrimmons's name from my notebook and hand it to her.

"We'll get out of your hair now," Ms. Whitman says. "Unless you have any more questions? And you're free to stop by the B&B anytime to make sure she didn't leave anything else you might want to have. She had quite the extensive library."

"That's very kind of you, Calliope. Maybe we could have coffee sometime."

Ms. Whitman grins. "I'd love that."

Mrs. Palmer turns to us, and her eyes have gone misty. "I want to thank you girls."

Edie shrugs, staring down at her boots. "We didn't do anything."

"But you did. Thank you for taking care of my mother's things, and for returning them." Mrs. Palmer looks at me now. "Mama was so happy when you and your dads moved in across the street. I think being around other black people reminded her of the life she'd shut off so long ago...the life that she missed."

28

ALL APOLOGIES

IT FEELS LIKE A BILLION YEARS SINCE LARAMIE AND I have sat next to each other at the Coleman Creamery counter, but when she asks me to meet her there on Saturday afternoon, I say yes right away.

She's waiting for me when I get there, watching Leif work. She looks over when the door moos, and smiles. "Hey."

"Hey," I say, sliding onto the stool she saved for me.

Leif is busy, but he asks what I want. Laramie almost drops her cone when I tell him to surprise me.

"What happened to butter pecan?" She sounds almost accusatory.

I shrug. "Life's too short to only try one ice-cream flavor."

"Have you brainwashed her?" Laramie says to Leif.

He just grins. A couple of minutes later, he hands me a cup of curry mint ice cream. Laramie stares in disbelief as I try it, declare it's good, and take another bite.

"Anything else you want to tell me? Do you suddenly eat meat now, too?"

I laugh. "Uh, no. But Denise and Tim and the baby left yesterday, so nobody will be cooking meat in our house, either."

"Do you miss them?"

"Yeah," I say. I don't tell her that I cried a little bit when I hugged Denise good-bye. I can still smell the patchouli as she leaned down, kissed my cheeks, and said, *I love you, sweet girl.* "The house was a little crowded, but Denise is, like, the best person ever. And they asked me to be the baby's godmother."

"Aren't we too young to be godparents?"

"I guess not."

Laramie glances around the shop, tucking a piece of hair behind her ears. She's been nervous ever since the rumor Nicolette spread, like she's always worried people are talking about her. The noise has died down over the past couple of days, but some people are still whispering at school. Edie overheard one of them in art class. "Gross," she said, rolling her eyes. "Don't you have anything better to talk about?"

When Leif walks away to help a customer, Laramie swivels toward me. Her toes tap against the leg of my stool. "I'm sorry."

I lick ice cream from the back of my spoon and look at her. Dad always says you're supposed to say what you're sorry for when you apologize to someone. I wonder if Laramie is going to say anything else.

"You were right about Nicolette. She's not a nice person. Even when it wasn't about me...she says mean things about people just because she can."

"So, why did you keep hanging out with her for so long?" I'm not trying to make her feel bad, but I actually want to know. It was like someone else took over my best friend's body for a few weeks.

"At first...I guess because she's an eighth grader and popular." Laramie sighs. "I wanted to see what it was like."

"But you're already popular!"

"I'm seventh-grade popular, not eighth-grade popular. There's a difference."

She's not wrong.

"But then, I started to like Gavin, and I could tell... I mean, I thought he liked me, too. He would look at me different from how he looked at everyone else. And he'd always hang back to talk to me about comics when we were in a group. Even after Nicolette told me she liked him, I kept hanging around them because...I don't know. I just thought it would work out, or whatever. I guess I should've known it was a bad idea when even Leif asked why I was hanging out with them."

"Did you have fun, at least? When you were with them?"

Laramie shrugs. "Sometimes. When they weren't so busy trying to be cool. But I missed you. I missed just being myself and people being okay with that." She clears her throat as she looks at me. "Are we still...you know...best friends?"

"Laramie." I set down my ice cream. "Of course

we are. I mean, Edie is my friend, too, and I wasn't just hanging out with her because you started hanging around Nicolette. She's a good friend and person. And not a poser."

"I shouldn't have said those things about her," she says. "But Nicolette was—"

"Can we make a pact?"

Laramie looks at me curiously.

"Can we try to go the rest of the month without saying Nicolette McKee's name? It's bad enough I have to look at her house every day." I shudder.

"Deal. Let's try for the rest of the year." She leans closer, her shoulder bumping mine. "Hey...can I have a bite of your curry mint? I've never tried it."

"You should really branch out more, Laramie," I say in a voice that sounds a whole lot like She-Who-Must-Not-Be-Named.

Laramie laughs as she dips her spoon into my cup of ice cream.

"Edie is coming over for our horror movie marathon this year," I say. "The day before Halloween, since her party is the night of. Want to come?"

Laramie makes a face. "Yes, but... do we have to watch *Jaws*?"

"We definitely do not have to watch *Jaws*."

"Will you make fun of me if I spend most of the marathon with my hand over my eyes?"

"Never," I say. "But I can't promise Elliott won't."

Laramie laughs again, and I realize how much I've missed this. Sitting with her at the creamery, making plans and giggling about nothing. It's nice.

Leif glances over as he passes by. He gives me a thumbs-up with a questioning look.

I nod, grinning. I'm pretty sure Laramie and I are going to be okay.

ALL HALLOWS' EVE

THE B&B IS TOTALLY DECKED OUT FOR HALLOWEEN.

Cobwebs cling to every surface outside, from the sign that now says WHITMAN INN to the eaves above the porch. Plastic skeleton bones are scattered around the yard, and two skulls sit on either side of the stairs leading to the porch. A ghoulish mask of a witch with bright red eyes and a screaming mouth sits over the door knocker.

"They really go all out, huh?" Laramie raises her eyebrows as I knock.

"It's Edie's favorite holiday."

Ms. Whitman opens the door, flooding the porch

with creepy whitish-blue light and even creepier music. She's dressed as Glinda the Good Witch, complete with a magic wand in hand.

"Hi, girls! Oh, you both look so good! Let me guess—a flapper," she says, pointing at Laramie's gold fringe dress and sequined headband. She stops as she assesses my costume. "I'm sorry, Alberta, I can't figure it out...."

"I'm Elliott," I say with a shrug. I'm wearing a version of his professor clothes with khaki pants, a button-down, and a sweater vest, plus glasses with fake lenses. And carrying a messenger bag that's holding one of his well-loved art books.

Ms. Whitman throws her head back and laughs. "I'm afraid to ask what he thinks."

Elliott couldn't help but laugh, too. Especially when he found out Dad and I had been planning it for weeks.

"They said they'll try to stop by later," I say.

"Is this a haunted house?" Laramie looks skeptically behind Ms. Whitman's pink-and-silver ball gown.

"Not quite. Just made to look like one," Edie's

mother says just as a terrifying scream plays over the recorded music.

Laramie stands extra close to me as we enter the B&B.

It takes me a minute to recognize the girl standing next to the snack table. She's wearing ruby-red slippers, a blue gingham dress with a lace-trimmed petticoat.... I get to her pigtails before I realize it's—

"Edie?"

She stuffs a piece of cheese in her mouth and waves as she chews.

"Oh my god," I say, walking over. "Your outfit..."

I've never seen her in anything besides black, sometimes with silver or white mixed in. But she is full-on Dorothy from *The Wizard of Oz*, and all the primary colors and pigtails make her look like a completely different person. She's still wearing lipstick, but it's red like her slippers instead of black.

"I know, right?" She shrugs. "Everyone probably expects me to be a witch or the Grim Reaper or something. This is totally going to freak them out." She gives my outfit a long look and says, "Are you supposed to be Elliott?"

I smile.

The three of us eat cheese and potato chips and drink punch, letting Ms. Whitman answer the door whenever trick-or-treaters stop by. I remember coming to the B&B for candy each year. Mrs. Harris would always exclaim over my outfit, even when it wasn't very original.

Slowly, kids from school start to show up, including Oliver, Fletcher, and Jamie. They're each dressed as a different superhero: Batman, Ant-Man, and Captain America. Oliver and Fletcher keep complaining and tugging at their masks, but Jamie looks totally comfortable hiding behind his.

Rashawn and Seth show up shortly after them, standing awkwardly in the doorway until Edie waves them over.

"Ooh, you invited *Rashawn*?" I tease her in a quiet voice.

She furiously blushes as we watch them walk our way. "Just as friends. I didn't think he'd come. Gavin's having a party, too, I guess. I figured he'd hang out with the eighth graders, but he said he'd stop by."

"What's up, Edie? Hey, Alberta. Hey, Laramie,"

Rashawn says, nodding at us as they approach. Seth flips his hair out of his face and I think that counts as his greeting.

They're not wearing costumes, because I guess eighth graders are too cool to wear them. But they don't look embarrassed to be here, and I notice Rashawn nodding approvingly at the decorations around the B&B.

Some parents stop in to say hi to Edie's mother when they drop off their kids for the party. The ones who are dressed in costumes usually stay, which thrills Ms. Whitman. At one point, I look up and see Mrs. Palmer standing in the foyer, hugging her. She's dressed in a pink poodle skirt with a silk scarf tied around her neck. I nudge Edie, who looks over and grins.

I wonder how it feels for Mrs. Palmer to be back in the house she grew up in. My dads couldn't have been more surprised when I told them what Edie and I found out about Mrs. Harris. I worried they might be mad at me for keeping it from them so long, but they told me they were proud of me for learning more about black history, and for returning the journals to the people who should have them. I told Denise when she video-called us one day to show us how Caleb was growing. She sounded proud, too, when she said I might be a budding journalist. That made me smile.

Edie and I walk over to say hi to Mrs. Palmer, but Edie is looking past her to the front door. I follow her gaze and can't believe what I see: Nicolette and Shauna are standing in the doorway, dressed in street clothes and looking around the B&B.

Edie stalks up to them, the angriest Dorothy I've ever seen. "What are you doing here?"

"Happy Halloween to you, too," Nicolette says with a tight smile.

"No, seriously, what are you doing here?"

"Well, I live next door, and I heard there was a party, so I thought I'd stop by and see what was up. Looks pretty creepy in here. Did you decorate?" The corner of her mouth turns up in a smirk.

Edie glares at her. "Real cute."

Nicolette gives me the once-over, still smirking. "You know, Alberta, you could've just worn your regular clothes if you wanted to dress like a dork."

Laramie walks up next to me then, staring hard at Nicolette. "Are you lost?"

"Oh, Laramie. Long time no see." Her eyes move over Laramie's costume. "Cool dress."

"What do you want, Nicolette?"

She rolls her eyes. "Why is everyone acting like it's such a big deal that I wanted to stop by my next-door neighbor's party?"

"Because you've been terrible to all of us?" Edie says in a clear voice.

"Oh, come on, new girl. I wasn't ever that bad to you."

"Not at all," Shauna murmurs, tossing her hair.

"Not to my face," Edie replies. "I know the things you said about me. And you can think what you want, but you couldn't hack it *one* day in Brooklyn. You couldn't even hack it one day outside of Ewing Beach."

"Please," Nicolette says, her hand shooting to her hip. "I'm probably the most cultured person in this room. In this entire *town*."

"I don't know about that," I say, "but you *are* the meanest. What is your actual problem?"

"Right now? That I'm standing here listening to a bunch of seventh graders act like they're better than me."

I step closer to her. "No, the problem is that *you've* always acted like you're better than everyone else. Especially me and my dads."

She rolls her eyes so hard I hope they get stuck there. "Cry me a river, Alberta. You shouldn't expect special treatment just because you're different."

"Special treatment? Since when is being polite to someone special treatment?" Laramie's voice gets louder the more she talks. "Alberta is right. You've always been a jerk to her, and we should've called you on it a long time ago."

"Aww, Laramie, that's too bad. I was going to see if you wanted to go to *Gavin's* house with us," she says, fluttering her eyelashes. "Remember him?"

"Not in a million years," Laramie mutters.

I look at Nicolette. "You know, I may be different from you or most people here, but at least I'm a good person. I can't change what I look like...and I don't want to. But you...The sad part is that you've been so mean for so long, I don't even think you know how to change."

Everyone is quiet then. Shauna looks down at the floor. Edie, Laramie, and I stare at Nicolette, whose face is so red she's practically the same color as Edie's ruby slippers.

Just then, Ms. Whitman bounces over in her ball gown. "Welcome to the party, girls. Can I—"

"They were just leaving, Mom," Edie says, walking toward Nicolette and Shauna until they start moving backward.

"But—"

"They have another party to go to." She's still walking, and Nicolette and Shauna are still backing up. Through the doorway and onto the porch until Edie yells "Bye!" and slams the door in their faces.

"Girls," Ms. Whitman says evenly, looking at all of us.

"I'll explain later, Mom. Trust me, we did the right thing."

"Oh my god," Laramie says as we head back to the food table. "Did that just happen?"

I only now realize how hard my heart is pounding in my chest. And how much lighter I feel after finally telling Nicolette what I think of her. I feel better than I have in *months*.

"Alberta, you were amazing," Edie says, handing me a glass of witch's brew. The big batch is sitting in a steaming cauldron—but it's really just ginger ale, juices, and sherbet with dry ice at the bottom.

"*Totally* amazing," Laramie says. "We should've done that years ago."

"You were both pretty amazing, too," I say, my cheeks hot. "We made a good team."

"Cheers to that," Edie says, and we all clink our cups of witch's brew before we drink them down.

"So, is this anything like your Halloween party in New York?" I ask, looking at all the people crammed into the B&B. I keep overhearing adults saying how nice it looks with the changes Ms. Whitman has made.

"Not really," Edie says. "But nothing can compare to that." She bites into a carrot stick and surveys the room. "I kept thinking maybe my dad would show up and surprise me tonight, since Halloween has always sort of been our thing."

"Maybe he will. The night isn't over."

Edie shakes her head. "No, he's in Brooklyn. He called from the party earlier, and everyone yelled hi to me in the background."

"Oh. Sorry," I say.

"No, it's okay. I guess...even though I sort of wanted him to be here, it's fine without him, you know? Like, I don't think a Ewing Beach Halloween is supposed to be exactly the same as a Brooklyn Halloween. And my mom tried really hard to make this a good one."

"Maybe she'll change her mind and you can go back to Brooklyn for Halloween next year," I say, adjusting my fake glasses.

"Maybe." Edie looks from me to Laramie to the guys, who are doing some kind of amateur superhero martial arts in the corner, and back to me again. "Or maybe I'll be right here in Ewing Beach with you guys. It's not so bad here."

"Yeah," I say. "It's not so bad at all."

Laramie grins. "Do we have to do a group hug now?"

"Let's not go wild," Edie says, laughing.

But I think back to what she said about it not being so bad here. Coming from Edie, I think that means she's starting to like it. Which is good.

Because now I can't imagine Ewing Beach without her.

ACKNOWLEDGMENTS

Middle-grade books have always held a special place in my heart. They're the stories that inspired me to become a writer and the books I still think about decades later. I'm grateful to my editor, Alvina Ling, for welcoming my first book for younger readers and helping me find my inner twelve-year-old. Thank you to Ruqayyah Daud for your organization and insightful comments (and for laughing at my jokes). To the rest of the team at Little, Brown Books for Young Readers, especially Victoria Stapleton, Alex Kelleher-Nagorski, Michelle Campbell, Christie Michel, Valerie Wong, Marisa Finkelstein, Kelley Frodel, and Marcie Lawrence: Thank you for always treating me and my books so well; I'm extremely grateful to work with you all. Thank you to Erin Robinson for another gorgeous work of art on my cover.

Thank you to Tina Dubois for pushing me to write the things that scare, thrill, and challenge me, and for supporting me through every stage; I am so unbelievably happy to know you. Thank you to Tamara Kawar for your enthusiasm and for sending my favorite emails. Thank you to my colleagues at Hamline University's MFAC program for providing me with constant inspiration, insight, and wit—I am endlessly awed by your talent and compassion. Thank you to my friends for being such exceptional people, and especially Nina LaCour for reading an early draft of this book and responding with your trademark warmth and thoughtfulness. And thank you most of all to my family for making books and reading such a fundamental part of my childhood; I am forever grateful for what storytelling has brought to my life.